FULLER THAN A
TICK

FAIRY TALES OF A TRAILER PARK QUEEN
BOOK 10

KIMBRA SWAIN

Kimbra Swain
Fuller than a Tick, Fairy Tales of a Trailer Park Queen, Book 10
©2018, Kimbra Swain / Crimson Sun Press, LLC
kimbraswain@gmail.com

Book Cover by: Audrey Logsdon
Formatting by: Crimson Sun Graphics
Editing by Carol Tietsworth: https://www.facebook.com/Editing-by-Carol-Tietsworth-328303247526664/

CRIMSON SUN PRESS

CHAPTER ONE

IN GENERAL, IT WAS KNOWN THAT WEARING WHITE AFTER Labor Day was a huge faux pas. However, two things in the South made this untrue. First, it stayed hot until December. Southerners could wear flip-flops to Christmas Dinner, then could wear them again to a New Year's Eve party. Secondly, weddings were always an exception to the rule.

The autumn leaves barely clung to the trees in the backyard where we were having the ceremony. The dapper groom wore brown slacks, a brown vest, and a baby blue plaid shirt. His groomsmen, including the handsome Levi Rearden, wore the same outfit minus the vest. They wore suspenders instead. Levi cussed the "damn things" when he put them on.

"Why on this green earth would any man want to wear these things?" he protested.

"I dunno, but it's cute," I replied. I thought maybe if I complimented him, he would ease up on the attire. Thankfully, it wasn't me or him getting married today. My proposed wedding date had slipped by unnoticed by most as we prepared to battle with the Wild Hunt. I preferred it that way.

"Just because you say you like it doesn't mean I will," he said. Then he cut his eyes to me with a grin.

"Uh-huh," I replied.

"Momma!" Winnie called from down the hallway. I walked to help her with her dress. She was serving as the flower girl, and she looked adorable. She had "experience" in the flower girl role since she had done the same for Amanda and Troy's wedding. However, this time her counterpart would be another young boy from school named Corbin. He and his family were raven shifters that had moved to town just after the Battle of Trailer Swamp. He was having trouble fitting in at school, so Ella asked him to be at the wedding to help include him. Winnie was less than enthusiastic about the "new kid."

Astor and Ella had requested to use the yard at my home to have the wedding, and I had granted the use of the house and yard without thinking much about it. They were like family to me, and I couldn't deny them. But as the day arrived, it hurt more than I thought it would. The dream and prophecy Dylan had had affected my emotions more than it should have.

Levi and I knew that our lives weren't written in stone or even in a songbook. We had to live it each day. In the last couple of weeks though, it seemed more like a possibility for us. I had to admit that we were too domestic. He took care of the kids like they were his. He waited on me hand and foot. During the day, he made the rounds in town to each business and person that he could. His dedication to the exiles was impressive.

Outside of a heightened sex drive, he hadn't suffered any other effects of being turned into a full-fairy. In fact, after it was all over, he thanked me for doing it. I had been selfish to ask, but I knew he felt the same way. If we were going to do this together, we might as well be in it for the long haul.

"You look very nice," he said.

"Thanks. Tabitha dropped this dress off the other day and

instructed me to wear it. That pretty much defines my part in the choosing," I said.

"Sounds like you didn't choose any of it," he replied.

"Exactly," I said.

The burgundy dress was made of lace with a tight burgundy sheath under it. The dress was longer than the under piece, so you could see my legs. The outfit came with tan shoes and a tan bag. I didn't carry a purse, and these heels were going to be a doozy in the grass outside. I couldn't complain. It was a nice outfit, and I didn't have to shop for it. My teacup necklace hung around my neck, and a cushion diamond ring flashed on my hand. Levi's ring.

After making sure Winnie was ready, I went downstairs to find Nestor sitting with William. They were playing with Aydan who was now running and talking up a storm.

"Momma, look," he said, holding up a toy for me to see.

"I see. What is it?" I asked.

"A dog," he replied.

"It's a wolf," I said.

He tilted his head back and howled. He'd seen Mark do it once when he was at the house playing with Winnie, and he mimicked the move every time someone mentioned a wolf.

"What's all that noise down here?" Levi asked as he came down the steps. "Is that you Aydan?"

"No!" Aydan said, hiding behind me.

"We can't have dogs in this house, because Rufus will get jealous!" Levi said.

"No!" Aydan cried out.

"I'm going to get you," Levi said.

Aydan took off running as fast as his chubby legs would carry him. Levi walked behind him, grabbing for him, but letting him get away. Finally, after a short chase, Levi picked him up and tossed him in the air. Aydan laughed so hard he couldn't catch his breath.

"Weevi! You silly," he said.

"Where did you learn that I was silly?" Levi asked.

Aydan pointed at me. The little devil.

"Oh, yeah? Your Momma said I was silly?" Levi asked.

"Yes," Winnie interjected. "She says it all the time, and you have to admit Uncle Levi, you are kinda silly."

"See," I said with a smile.

"I can't say that's a bad thing," Levi said.

"Not at all," William agreed.

Astor walked out of the hallway in his get-up with a scowl on his face. "What's wrong?" I asked.

"I'm nervous," he said, wringing his hands.

I walked over to him and kissed him on the cheek. "You look very handsome, Astor. She is a very lucky woman to have such a wonderful man," I said.

He sighed. "Thank you, Grace."

"It will be fine. Remember to breathe. If you pass out, I'm going to video it on my phone," I said. Astor paled at the prospect.

"No, she won't, Copper Top," Levi said. "She doesn't know how to use the camera on her phone."

"I do too!" I said.

"The video camera?" he asked.

"Maybe. I'm sure I could figure it out," I said.

There was a light tap on the door, and Luther peeked into the room. "It's time," he said.

"Alright, Little Bird. You are with me," I said. Aydan ran over to me, and I took his hand as William and Nestor made their way outside to the wedding area, we had set up near the forest that led to my stone circle.

"Grace," Levi said just before I left.

"Yeah?" I said looking back at him.

"You really do look beautiful," he said.

"And you really do look handsome. I wasn't saying it just to

4

make you feel better about it," I smiled, then slipped out the door with my little date.

CHAPTER TWO

AYDAN SAT HAPPILY NEXT TO ME AS THE CROWD BEGAN TO settle into their seats. Matthew Rayburn stood before the crowd under an arch made of vines. He had replaced the cloth binding over his eyes with a nice pair of aviator sunglasses. Kady guided him to the position, then took a seat on the front row next to Caleb Martin.

The procession began with the men walking out with Astor Knight. I was glad he had chosen the last name. Now he could properly claim Ella Jenkins as his own. Aydan stood up in the seat next to me and waved at Levi who grinned as he waved back. He picked up a guitar from the stand behind him. Astor had purchased a new one for him. The neck and base were covered in Celtic knots, and the tree of life covered the hole at the bottom. Even though he didn't need it anymore, Levi gushed for weeks over the new guitar. He agreed to play Canon in D on the guitar for the wedding march.

When he started to play, a collective sigh rolled through the crowd. He played both the guitar and the tattoo. A one-man duet. I'd heard him practicing it, and it sounded wonderful. He truly had a talent for music beyond just your normal good musician. I could see him on a stage as one of those rock stars. The women would faint and swoon, and it would be well deserved.

A young woman with dark brown hair walked down the aisle in a light blue chiffon dress. I had met her a few days ago when Ella brought her by the house. Crystal Marie had strange blue eyes that shifted colors when she moved her head. She and Ella had been mates in college. They met at the university and each had quickly found out that the other wasn't normal. Recently, Crystal moved to town and had sworn her allegiance to the local alpha. We had decided it was necessary for all shifters to follow Troy. Even Dominick Meyer, who had hidden his alpha status, had sworn the oath. Troy trusted him enough to make him his second in command behind Amanda.

I looked across the crowd, and I saw Dominick sitting with Troy and Amanda. A restless Mark shifted back and forth in his seat. Amanda was trying to calm him, but Dominick picked him up, setting him on his lap. Mark stopped moving around and watched the procession. I knew he was looking for a particular little Phoenix.

Dominick hadn't approached me again, but he would give me a smile from across the room. Or a polite greeting when he did police work with Troy and it brought them by the office. He still was handsome, and I knew he was still interested. Another day and another time, I might have been, but not considering the current circumstances.

Crystal continued her walk. She was a were-bobcat which I'd never seen until she showed me her shift. She was a beautiful creature. Feline and elegant. Even in human form, she walked down to the altar with air in her step.

Behind her, Winnie stepped out with Corbin who looked more afraid of Winnie than the crowd. They walked down the aisle slowly as Winnie dropped petals along the way. I'd prepared myself to put out any fires, but she made it down to her spot without incident.

Ella appeared at the back of the seating arrangement through a portal created by Tennyson's sword. She stepped through with Eugene Jenkins and his lion, Chaz Leopold. They stood on either side of her to walk her down the aisle. Chaz held a white handkerchief to his eyes as he boohooed like a baby.

The bride kept her eyes on her groom, and he watched her in awe. It was just as a committed marriage should be. She looked radiant, and he looked happy to stand in her shadow. Tabitha had gushed about the dress saying that Jenny had picked it out for her. I only knew the details because I listened to them twitter about it like two biddies. The mermaid dress flared out at the bottom and the entire thing was covered in lace. She carried blue hydrangea and baby's breath in her bouquet. I was told that Chaz made all the bouquets. They were lovely.

It seemed the entire town had shown up for the wedding. It was nice to celebrate a new beginning.

As she reached the front, Levi's song ended. He immediately looked to me. I nodded for his job well done. The smile didn't reach his lips, but it twinkled in his eyes.

The ceremony was beautiful. More traditional than Amanda and Troy's Druid ceremony. Chaz cried. Astor didn't faint. Winnie didn't set anything on fire, and Aydan managed to be quiet for about 20 minutes.

"You may kiss the bride," Matthew said, smiling at the couple.

Astor leaned over to kiss Ella's lips when I saw Levi wince.

"*Someone has crossed the ward,*" he said.

"*Now?*" I asked in frustration.

His eyes darted behind us.

"Halt!" a deep voice resonated from the back of the audience.

"Really?" I grunted.

Betty was sitting next to me, and she grabbed up Aydan, handing him to Luther.

Standing up, I spun around to face a familiar being.

"Marshall! We are trying to have a wedding here. You are welcome to join us," I said.

Tennyson stood up from the crowd, facing the centaur as did Troy. Troy's hands fell to his hips where he wore Driggs. I felt Levi approaching me from behind.

"Greetings, Queen of the Exiles. I bring a message from Astor's mother," he said.

"Of course, you do. Go ahead," I prompted. We had met Marshall on our visit to Summer. He was the captain of the centaur guard for Rhiannon's castle. In Summer, he was congenial. However, now I felt a sense of urgency as if he were compelled to be here. Looking at him through my sight, I saw the collar around his human neck. It swirled with the green power of the Summer Queen.

"Queen Rhiannon forbids this marriage to happen. She has informed me to tell you that if you allow it, then she will come to take her son back by force," he said.

"Oh please, send her here. I'd love to kill her inside the Vale she created," I said. Turning back to Astor and Ella, I said, "Kiss her."

He nodded, then completed the ceremony with the kiss.

Marshall shook his head. "She will not be pleased. Perhaps if they do not consummate the marriage," he suggested.

"Oh, it's going to be consummated!" Ella said behind me. The crowd snickered.

"Those two people are free folk here. We don't go by the Queen of Summer's commands. I'm in charge, and they are allowed to do as they wish. And if Rhiannon wants to bring her skinny ass into my town, remind her that we defeated the Hunt.

I'm sure she's heard about that by now. I'd love to kill her here," I said.

"There will be consequences," Marshall said.

"Ain't scared. Bring it," I taunted. If Rhiannon was going to be rude enough to interrupt a wedding, I was not going to worry about my manners either.

Levi eased up behind me. I could hear the light humming of the sword in his hand. Marshall's eyes darted to it, then back to me.

"So, it's true. You gave the bard the Great Sword," he said.

"I did," I replied.

He huffed, and it sounded more horse than human. "Your love for these people will be your downfall," he said. "If you are truly a Queen, you could do this on your own."

I leaned back on Levi and grinned. "But I'd much rather do it with them."

"*Do what exactly?*" Levi asked.

"*Hush,*" I replied.

"I will tell the queen," he said.

"Marshall," I called to him as he turned to walk away.

"I could take that collar off of you, and you could stay here," I offered.

He looked at me with sad eyes and replied, "I will not forsake my Queen." He nodded in thanks, then trotted off into the woods.

"Well, wasn't that thrilling," I said enthusiastically. Perhaps a little sarcastically, just to lighten the mood. When I faced Levi, he was grinning again. I shook my head at him before he could imply anything else. "Let's party!"

The crowd cheered, then made their way to the tent set up behind the house for a lively reception.

CHAPTER THREE

Wendy, Ford, and a group of gypsies provided lively music for dancing and celebrating. The children ran around playing in the yard. Winnie's dress had singe marks on it. I wasn't sure what she had tried to burn or tried not to burn, but it looked like the dress got the brunt of it. Aydan sat in my lap clapping with the music.

"Momma," he said.

"Yes?" I answered.

"Musey," he said which translated meant music.

"Yep, the gypsies are playing music. Do you like it?" I asked.

"Yesh," he said with a slight lisp.

Levi walked up with a cup of punch for me, and a cup of something for Aydan with a lid and straw. "You want some cake?" he asked.

"No, I'm fine," I replied, as he took a seat in the folding chair next to me.

"Well, all in all, it was a good wedding. Minus the centaur," he said.

"Wasn't that kind of strange though?" I asked.

"How so? You had to guess that Rhiannon would try to put her two cents in," he said.

"Yeah, but I think maybe there was more to it," I said.

"I'm sure there was," he said. "Fairies are manipulative. She's playing a game."

"Okay, now. You are just as much fairy as the rest of us now," I said.

"I like to think I've still got a little human in me," he smiled.

"You do. Way too much," I said.

He laughed as Jenny came and sat down at the roundtable with us. She had a plate with a slice of cake on it. "Oh, my goodness, this cake is magical," she said.

"It probably is. Luther made it," I replied.

"I don't care who made it. It's amazing," she said.

"Are you and Tennyson going to tie the knot?" Levi asked.

"Yea, about the same time you and Grace get married," she said with an evil grin.

I almost snorted punch out of my nose. Levi laughed at her while I tried to find a napkin on the table. He handed me one, and I wiped my mouth.

"You know, I'm the only one around here that can say such things and get away with it," I said, teasing her back. She loved irritating me about Levi even though he and I had reached an agreement on the whole "wedding prophecy" thing.

"Apparently not," she grinned with icing on her lips.

Tennyson unbuttoned his jacket and sat next to her. She picked up a small piece of cake on a fork offering it to him. He shook his head no, then looked over to us.

"Are you concerned?" he asked.

"About Rhiannon?" I asked back.

"Yes," he replied.

"Not really. I doubt she would come here knowing she could

cease to exist if she died here. She's the one that created this cursed place," I said.

"Actually, killing her here might be the only way to break the curse," Levi said.

"You sure about that?" I asked.

"No, but it makes sense. I've been reading the spell book that we found in Mable's things. There were a lot of curses there towards the end of the book," he said. "The way to reverse them often lies in the caster removing them."

"I'm not sure we can get her to volunteer that after I let her grown son get married to a lovely woman," I said. Over Jenny's shoulder, I could see Astor and Ella immersed in each other on the dance floor. The gypsies were playing a slower song, and the newlyweds swayed to the music in each other's arms.

Throughout the day I had pushed away images of my own wedding that never happened. I had never been keen on the idea in the first place, but now that it hadn't happened, I had missed the what could have been.

"*Grace,*" Levi's voice echoed in my head.

"Sorry, got distracted," I said, looking back to Jenny.

"They make a beautiful couple," she said. "Are they going to live here?"

"No! Thank goodness. They are building a house on the other side of my property. It flanks the far side of the stone circle," I said. "It's almost finished. Remy has been working on it. In the meantime, they are going to live in one of the small houses in Neverland estates."

Remy and Tabitha walked up to join us at the table.

"Well, speak of the devil," I said.

"Grace, you talkin' about me again?" Remy said in his N'awlins drawl.

"Yep," I replied.

"I've told you. It's over between us. I'm in love with my doctor here," he said as he wrapped an arm around Tabitha. She blushed and shook her head at him.

"Well, darn," I said.

"That's okay, Grace. I hear that Troy's Beta still has his eye on you," Jenny offered with her hand over her mouth to conceal the wad of cake she was chewing on. Levi grunted, and Jenny giggled.

"He hasn't spoken to me since that day in Hot Tin," I said.

"I bet he would dance with you," Jenny teased. Levi became more uncomfortable as the tease continued.

"I'm not in the dancing mood," I said flatly, trying to shut it down.

"That's too bad," she said as she licked the icing off her fork. Tennyson watched her lustfully.

"Stop that," he grunted. She licked it again watching him shift in his seat.

"Good grief. Get a room," I said.

"I think I will," she replied. "Goodnight y'all."

Tennyson jumped up to offer his hand. She took it, and they walked back toward the front of the house where everyone had parked their vehicles. I knew that Stone and Bronx were out there waiting on them. I had already sent each of them a piece of cake.

Bramble flew up, then landed on the table in front of me.

"My queen," he squeaked. "The children are playing too close to the woods considering night is upon us."

"I'll get it," Levi said, standing up. "Show me where, Bramble."

"Right this way, my King," Bramble replied.

Bramble and Briar were the only ones that called Levi King. Everyone else treated him with respect as a leader and formidable force, but not as a King. I feared that the only thing that would gain him that title would be a marriage.

"How are you and he getting along?" Tabitha asked.

"Just fine," I replied.

"You sure about that?" she asked.

"What are you getting at?"

"I dunno. It just seems like something has changed between you," she replied.

"We reached an agreement," I said.

"Do tell," she smiled. Remy leaned back in his chair waiting for me to respond.

"We talked about it, and we both agree that thinking about Dylan's prophecy will only hinder our progress here in Shady Grove. We are planning an attack on Winter, and the last thing we need to worry about is a dream that may or may not come true. If it happens, it happens. If it doesn't, it doesn't," I explained.

"If it doesn't, it will kill him," she said. Remy poked her in the side. "Ow!"

"Grace, what she means is, there are consequences for him if you decide that you don't love him," Remy said.

"That's just it. I do love him. Isn't that right, Aydan?" I replied.

"Aydan!" Aydan said mimicking his name.

"Yes, Aydan, I love Levi more than any other man in this town. For now, it's enough," I said.

"And when it isn't enough?" Tabitha asked.

"I don't know," I replied. The conversation had made me uncomfortable. I began to look for a way out, but the one that approached wasn't what I was thinking about.

"Good afternoon, everyone," Dominick said to the table.

We greeted him when he turned to me. I groaned inside because I knew it was coming.

"Grace, I would be honored if you would dance with me," he said.

I sighed, then said, "I'm sorry. I'm not really in the dancing mood tonight. Thank you for your offer."

"Raincheck, perhaps?" he asked with a wide smile. His green eyes flickered with the animal inside of him.

"Maybe," I replied trying to be polite.

"The wedding was very nice, and your home is beautiful," he said. "Have a good evening." He backed away slowly without breaking eye-contact with me. It was a bold move, and he held it without looking away. It wasn't anything like he had done in the bar with me the first time we met.

Unfortunately for him, he backed right into Levi.

"Hello, Dominick," Levi said with the worst fake smile I'd ever seen.

"Oh, hey, Levi. Good party. I'm heading out," Dominick said, then rushed out of the tent.

Levi's eyes locked on me. A scowl painted his handsome scarred face.

"Uh-oh," Tabitha muttered.

I rolled my eyes, as Levi marched up. He took the seat next to me again without a word.

"How are the children?" I asked.

"Away from danger," he replied shortly.

"Good," I said.

A cheer went up from the crowd as Astor and Ella got ready to leave. Levi reached for Aydan who went straight to him. He stood with him on his hip, offering his hand to me. I took it, and we walked out together to the line of waiting friends and family.

Astor and Ella left with a flurry of love. I sighed pushing the dark thoughts away. Astor made eye-contact with me right before he slipped into the truck we bought for him. He nodded in thanks and I smiled because my ginger knight was about to have a night to remember.

CHAPTER FOUR

LEVI HELPED WITH THE CLEAN-UP OUTSIDE WHILE I GOT
Aydan and Winnie put to bed.

"How did you do this to this dress?" I asked pulling the burnt
dress off over her head. Her brown hair flared out with static electricity and she giggled.

"I didn't mean to do it," she sighed.

"Luther has been teaching you to control it," I said. "Right?"

"Yes, and I can control it," she said. "Most of the time."

"Most of the time isn't good enough, Winnie. You've got to
work harder. Did you get angry at someone?" I asked knowing that
when she got mad at me once before she had lost control.

"Maybe," she said.

"Who?" I asked.

"That boy," she snorted.

"Wynonna Riggs, what boy?"

"Corbin," she huffed.

"Did you burn him?" I asked.

"No, Mark tackled me before I let it go on him," she said.

"Why in the world did you want to burn him?" I asked. I knew there had been a time or two in my life where a man made me mad enough to want to freeze his dick off, but I didn't think that would be a good example to share with Winnie. Besides, she was only seven. What could a little boy do to piss her off so badly?

Just a couple of weeks ago we had a birthday party filled with rainbows and unicorns. It was a glittery fun occasion without a fire incident. In fact, there hadn't been an incident in almost three weeks.

"He said bad things," she said.

"What kind of bad things?" I asked.

"He said that Mark and I were boyfriend and girlfriend. I tried to tell him we were just friends, but Corbin kept on and on and on and wouldn't stop," she said.

"So, you burned him?" I asked.

"No, Momma. I just got mad. The fire stuff just happened," she replied. "I'm very sorry. I didn't burn him. Just my dress. Mark kept me from doing it."

"Well, good for Mark. Winnie, honey, you've got to be more careful," I said.

"I know, Momma," she replied. I kissed her goodnight and shut the door to her room. "Momma?"

"Yes, Winnie?"

"Will you make sure Uncle Levi gives me a goodnight kiss?" she asked.

"Of course," I replied. I wouldn't have to remind him. He never forgot.

"*The princess wants her kiss,*" I said.

"*On my way,*" he replied.

I walked down the hallway to Aydan's room. Nestor sat in the rocking chair with the little man asleep on his lap. He wasn't so little anymore though. He was growing way too fast, and it made my heart ache to see it.

"How's Winnie?" he asked.

"She got mad at a boy and almost burned him, but Mark stopped her," I said. "I need to thank him for watching out for her."

"He's attached to her," Nestor said.

"How does that work with wolves? Can they choose a mate this early?" I asked.

"Yes, but I don't think it's gone that far. He's very protective though. I think it's a good thing for her," he said.

I sighed. Winnie was seven. The last thing I wanted to consider was her mating. Ugh.

"Come on, Little Bird," I said lifting the little chunk off Nestor's lap.

"He was very good today," Nestor said.

"He's always good," I said as I kissed his cheek, then laid him down in the toddler bed we recently bought. The crib wouldn't hold him anymore. So, we moved up a notch on the bed scale.

"Night, night, Momma," he muttered.

"I love you, Aydan," I said.

Nestor and I slipped out into the hallway. When I looked him in the eye, I knew he was worried about me.

"I'm fine," I said.

Levi bounded up the steps, looked at us for a moment, then rushed into Winnie's room.

"You sure?" Nestor persisted.

"I'm sure. It was a gorgeous wedding. Everyone had a blast. I'm good," I said.

He hugged me tightly. "See you tomorrow," he said as he left me alone with Levi and the children.

"Night, Princess," Levi said as he closed her door.

"Everything cleaned up outside?" I asked.

"Just about. I need your help with something," he said.

"Okay," I replied, following him down the steps.

"There are some serving plates out here that I don't know where they go," he said.

"Why are you lying to me?" I asked.

He stopped just before opening the back door. "Because," he said.

When he opened the door, the backyard was completely devoid of all the wedding paraphernalia, except the tent and the floor. I sighed shaking my head at him.

"Don't even. It is traditional to dance at a wedding, and you didn't. It was a slight to the couple. I'm giving you a chance to make it up," he said, grinning like a fool. He offered me his hand, but I didn't take it.

"I wasn't lying to Dominick when I told him I wasn't in the mood," I said.

"I don't care. You are going to dance with me even if I have to make you," he countered, lifting the eyebrow under his scar.

If I didn't relent, he was serious, because he'd use his power over me to make me do it. I wasn't going to bed before I danced with him. Occasionally, I knew that I had to give something to him. He needed it, and I owed it to him for his devotion and loyalty. It was like nourishment for his love-talker soul. Placing my hand in his, I allowed him to escort me to the center of the tent.

Power swirled around us as he pulled it to play his tattoo.

One arm on my waist. Another in my hand. He began to lead me around the floor.

"It might be condescending, but I was proud of you tonight," he said.

Quirking my face sideways to him, he laughed. "Sounds condescending," I smirked.

"You allowed them to have the wedding here because you love them. Despite your own pain and loss, you put that aside for them. It's pretty awesome of you, Grace," he said.

"I couldn't tell them no," I said, trying to avoid getting choked up.

The hand around my waist pulled me closer to him, and we no longer moved around the floor. We just swayed to the light tones of his guitar. I had watched women in this town for over a year dream of getting a moment like this with Levi, and he was giving it to me. The one person who couldn't love him as he wanted. I loved Levi for this, and for so many other things, but the thought of being with him caused more pain than pleasure. Until that ratio changed, we were both shit outta luck.

"Don't over think it, Grace," he said. "We are just dancing."

"It feels like more than dancing," I said. He couldn't help but smile.

"Maybe it is," he said. "But we made an agreement. One that I intend to honor."

"This is honoring our agreement?" I asked.

"Absolutely. I told you. It was a wedding, and you should have danced at it. I'm just giving you the opportunity to make up for your mistake," he said.

"They will never know," I said.

"Sure. I can't wait to tell Astor you danced with me," he said.

I wrenched my hand from his and slapped him on the shoulder. "Levi!" I said, laughing because I couldn't help it. He laughed, and to my surprise, the guitar continued to play. He had more concentration than I thought. He took my hand again, bringing my palm to his lips.

"I love you, Grace," he said, then kissed my palm.

Suddenly, I was in sensory overload. The tingle of the kiss, the magic of the music, and the sincerity in his voice. It was like I was drowning in it. I stepped away from him to break the intensity.

"I'm sorry," I said. "It was too much."

The guitar stopped. "No, I'm sorry," he said, hanging his head.

I couldn't leave him like this, even though I wanted to run. I put my hand over his scar on his cheek. "I think that you have more power than you know. From your father's side. Your words, actions, and magic bring an intensity that I couldn't bear. It's not your fault, Levi."

"I shouldn't have said that," he said.

Lifting his eyes to mine, I said, "I love you, too. You know that, right?"

"Yeah, but it's not the same," he said with a touch of broody. It made me grin. He shook his head, knowing what had caused it.

"I should go to bed," I said.

"Yeah, I'll just get the lights turned off and put up the wards for the night," he said.

I kissed him on the cheek and left him alone on the dance floor. I felt his pain. I hurt, too. Not just for the hole in my heart, but for the longing in his.

CHAPTER FIVE

Troy sat across from my desk with Amanda by his side. We talked about Winnie and Mark. Specifically, the incident with Corbin.

"I'm thankful he is so protective of her, but I don't want to see him get hurt," I said. "She's so powerful, and we haven't tamed it yet."

"You might not ever tame it. Sometimes things like this are hard to determine," Amanda said. "Mark is tough, and he adores her. Don't worry about him."

"Don't you worry that he's too attached? They are seven!" I said.

"He could very well become so attached to her that he would want her for a mate. Usually, males don't do that until they're teens. I think we don't have to worry about that for now. A wolf is protective by nature. He's just protecting what he considers to be his, even if she doesn't see it that way," Amanda said.

"Ugh. I don't even want to think about mating," I said.

"It won't be long, Grace," Troy said. "Kids these days grow up fast."

"I'm glad to know that they will grow up at the same rate. Aydan will surpass Winnie next year," I said. "I don't know what I'm going to do with either of them. Little clap of thunder likes to show off sometimes."

"He's still doing that?" Troy asked.

"Yeah, it's pretty impressive, but on a sunny day, it's sort of strange," I said. "He only does it when I'm upset."

"Well, then don't be upset," Amanda said.

"In general, I'm not, but I have my moments," I said.

"The last few months have been rough. That's completely understandable," Amanda replied.

"I suppose, but I don't want to use that as an excuse. We have too much to do," I said.

"Which is my cue to leave the two of you alone," Amanda said.

She kissed Troy goodbye then left on four legs instead of two. Troy and I needed to discuss our next move against my Uncle in the Otherworld.

"Before we get started, I want to apologize for Dominick," he said. "I don't think he means any harm. He's been very patient. I guess he just thought he could get you to dance at the wedding."

It had been a few days since the wedding, and Levi and I went on about our duties avoiding the topic of our dance. He had so much to do now that he was the mayor. People from around town would call him at all times of the night. It was almost like anything that Troy and his force didn't take care of, it was left up to Levi to cover. From getting old trunks out of people's attics to delivering a meal to a neighbor, he'd become Shady Grove's errand boy. I particularly hated it. It kept him away from home and his family. Our family.

However, he was damn good at it. He loved being the one to help everyone whenever they needed it. He was gone today out to the cottages near Pine Creek Road to patch up some roofs with Remy's construction crew. They had finished up on Astor and

Ella's house, and they needed to move on to some repairs that were needed around town. Remy liked having Levi there. It made the citizens calmer and more willing to help since most of them didn't know Remy's crew. Fairies, even in Shady Grove, could be skittish to new people, even if it was other fairies.

"I wasn't offended. I'm sorry that I'm just not to the point of letting anyone in," I said.

"Even then, there's Levi," he said.

"Yes, then there's Levi," I responded. As fuckable as Dominick looked, he wasn't Levi or Dylan. Nor would he ever be. "Let's talk about this raid."

"Yes, I got the details from Tennyson, but he wanted me to show you the map to make sure we got the locations correct," he said. "He hoped you would remember this part of the castle."

I'd been all over my father's castle. I knew every inch of it. Troy unfolded a piece of paper on my desk depicting the site for our raid. I looked over the details. They seemed to be in order except for one thing.

"This room has 12 pillars, not 10," I said.

"Tennyson wondered if you would catch that. It seems that your Uncle had two of the pillars knocked out and has two ogres that perform the support duties for the roof in that area. A punishment for treason," he said.

"Why don't they just let it fall on his ass," I said.

"Because they are blocks of ice," he replied.

"Oh," I said. It actually sounded like something my father would do. The only caveat here was that the ogres probably didn't commit treason. My uncle was just hateful like that.

"I don't think what we are looking for is in this room though," I said. "Seems I remember *it* in another place."

"Get started without me?" Tennyson asked as he strolled into the room. I'd added more chairs in the office because we tended to have our war council meetings here. Tennyson eased back into "his" chair in the corner of the room.

"We had just started. Covered a few personal items," I said.

"Where's Levi?" Tennyson asked.

"We don't need him here," I said.

"For this we do," Tennyson replied.

"I'm sure I can handle our discussion," I said as I started to get irritated.

Tennyson smiled, then gently replied, "Grace, you are more than capable, but he's got to start using that sword. It's a huge key to this whole plan. Call him."

"*Levi*," I reached out to him.

"*Yeah?*" he quickly answered.

"*Tennyson says you need to be here for this meeting*," I said.

"*On my way*," he replied.

Honestly, he'd been distant since the wedding. I told myself that my reaction to his absence had more to do with my self-centered need for attention, but I knew better. Hearing movement on the other end of the trailer, I knew he was here. We had converted the other bedroom into his mayor's office. He kept spare clothes and other necessities there.

When he walked into the room, he was rubbing a towel in his hair. I could tell he had put on a fresh shirt.

"Sorry. I was on a roof," he said. "Remy is a slave driver."

"Did you use the sword?" Tennyson asked.

"No, I didn't," he replied. "But you don't need to worry about it. I've got that part of the plan."

"Fine," Tennyson said. It was clear that he didn't believe Levi, but I wasn't going to get in the middle of that argument. I trusted Levi more than Tennyson. There was no need to pick sides.

"You stink," I said.

He grinned at me. "You wanna shower with me?" he asked.

"No," I replied. "Keep dreamin', Dublin."

"Never stopped," he said. *"Thanks for changing the subject."*

"Any time," I replied.

"Do I really stink?" he asked.

"I don't want to find out. Stay on that side of the room, please."
He shook his head at me but leaned on the wall near the door. I
didn't know what was worse. The thought of sweaty, sexy Levi or
the thought of just showered, wet Levi. Either way, I had to push it
out of my mind.

"Tennyson, this artifact wasn't housed in this room," I said
pointing at the 10-pillar room map.

"It's there," he said.

"No, Father kept it in his chambers," I said.

"Yes, but when it was clear that things were changing, he hid
most of his valuables in places all over the castle. I know your
uncle tore this room apart looking for Goswhit," he said.

Goswhit was my father, King Arthur's helmet. He had a whole
set of named armor and weapons including Excalibur, his sword,
which now belonged to my bard. He'd proven himself more than
worthy to carry it. The helmet had a great power like all my
father's toys. However, I wasn't sure why this one had topped
Tennyson's wish list.

"And why is the helmet worth this dangerous infiltration of the
enemy?" I asked.

"Did your father never tell you what it does?" Tennyson asked.

"No, but I'm sure you and your wealth of knowledge will," I
smirked.

He shook his head, but explained, "Goswhit, while on earth,
was nothing more than a helmet that protected your father's head.
It cannot be pierced by any means including magic. However,
when your father became King of the Unseelie, the helm allowed
him to control the borders of the land. He could see far and wide
across the vastness that is the Otherworld. If on the outside, the
helm can see in. It sees all."

"With the helmet, we can see what Brockton is doing so we will know when it is best to attack," Levi surmised.

"Yes," Tennyson confirmed. "But he could use it to destroy the veil between worlds."

That caught my attention. Destroying the veil between the Otherworld and the human world would allow all sorts of bad things to cross over unimpeded.

"What kind of resistance are we looking at?" I asked.

"My sources say that there is an army of wild that covers the outsides of the castle, but inside, your father's private guard now serve Brockton," Tennyson said.

I stood up to move to the window. Looking out into the fall afternoon, I thought about my father's private guard. A mass of two hundred harpies. They weren't loyal to my uncle or my father for that matter. They were protectors of the throne and whoever sat upon it. Cursed to that occupation when the old ones ruled the Otherworld, they had multiplied their numbers even though every single one of them was female. They shifted much like other fairies but preferred to stay in their half-bird, half-woman forms. Birdies with big breasts. Every one of them had big honkers. It was like Hooters met a wildlife aviary and had little harpy babies.

Remembering more of my time before I was banished, I thought about the time I overheard my brother trying to convince one to shift to female so he could explore her anatomy. He had tried to make it sound like a science experiment. She didn't fall for it.

"Speaking of Finley," I said.

"We didn't mention Finley," Levi said, knowing that my thoughts had strayed.

"Right," I scowled. He winked at me. Bastard. "Anyway. I'm supposed to meet with Finley and the white witches tonight to see what level of help we can expect from them."

"Are you okay with Riley and Finley?" Tennyson asked.

Taking a deep breath, I tried to keep my answer mature. "It's his choice," I said.

"But if she steps out of line, we will take her down," Levi filled in the blank for me.

"Yes, we will," I said.

"Perhaps she is trying to make things right?" Troy interjected.

"Is that your instinct on it?" I asked. Wolves could smell a person's intentions. Troy had explained to me, that it was harder to smell that from a fairy, but he had gotten pretty good at it living in Shady Grove for so long.

"It is," he said. "I find nothing in her that is false. Not anymore."

"She will be a good ally if she proves that she is with us," Tennyson said. "I've had to make deals with former enemies. You can do it too, Grace."

"I'm not you," I said.

"I am aware," he replied.

Deep breath. Mature. "I will try."

CHAPTER SIX

AFTER TENNYSON AND TROY LEFT, LEVI TOOK TENNYSON'S chair.

"I'm not sure I can work with her," he admitted.

"Me either," I sighed. "She did help protect the vault with the kids in it though."

"Yes. It's hard not to think that she doesn't have some secondary agenda, and she's using Finley to make it seem like she's legit," he said. "The only thing I can figure is she's so pissed off at her mother about Jeremiah's death that she will do whatever it takes to see that Rhiannon suffers."

"Perhaps," I said. I didn't want to talk about Riley. I wanted to talk about us. "I've missed you at home."

He blinked, allowing my words to sink in. "Grace, I'm home every night," he countered.

"Your body is there," I said.

"I'm just giving you space. I crossed a line," he said.

"There are no lines between us," I replied. "At least, I don't want there to be any."

He shook his head. "No, I have to have boundaries for myself," he huffed. Almost a brood. "I carried it too far. We could have had a nice dance, but I opened my big, fat mouth."

"Do you take it back? What you said?" I questioned.

"Of course not," he said, lowering his head.

"Levi, I know how you feel. You didn't have to say it for me to know. It's in your actions every day. I see it in your face now, but it's causing you pain. That is the last thing I want," I said.

The more I thought about our dance, the more I realized how sweet and wonderful it was that he took the effort to get me out of my shell. It was just like him. People always say I'm the fairy with a heart, but now that Levi was a full-blooded fairy, he had me beat in that category.

"Yes, but I made you uncomfortable. I won't get ahead of myself again," he said.

"Stop separating yourself from me. I'm kinda used to having you close. I'm selfish like that," I smiled. He tilted his head up to see if I was joking. I saw the light return to his denim eyes.

"Really? Tell me more about that," he said.

"Look at the time. We've got to go meet your ex-girlfriends!" I said with a smile.

"Ugh. Can we please stop calling them that? Kady is with Caleb, and Riley is with your brother," he said.

"It doesn't negate the fact that you swapped gravy with both of them," I said.

"Grace, please," he brooded.

"Look at it this way. My brother and Caleb are getting your sloppy seconds," I smiled.

He dropped the scowl, then erupted in laughter. "That's right! My castaways," he laughed.

"Or you could take them all back and have your own harem like my father. It would be a kingly thing to do," I suggested.

"I'm pretty sure I'm the complete opposite of your father," he said.

"Which is a plus in my book," I said.

"Well, while you chauffeur me over to the RV park, you can tell me more about the selfish pluses in your book," he teased.

"Chauffer? I think not." I threw the keys from the top of my desk at him. He reached up and caught them without flinching. He was getting faster. Fairy reflexes. "You are driving me."

"Fine. Come on, Miss Daisy," he smirked. I looked for something else to throw at him, but I couldn't find anything that I wanted to break.

Wendy invited us into her RV. Rumor had it that Fordele and some of the other gypsies were upset with her for going against their vote to stay out of the Battle at Trailer Swamp. She had assured me that everything would be fine. However, stepping inside of her RV, it was devoid of the items that I'd seen before that clearly belonged to Ford.

"Are you alright?" I asked.

"I assure you, Grace. All is well," she said.

"Okay. Well, let's do this," I said.

When Levi and I entered, the two chattering voices of Riley and Kady ceased. Finley jumped up from the seating area to hug me.

"Glory, you look well today," he said. "Levi."

"Fin," Levi said, extending his hand to my brother. Finley shook it.

"Please have a seat," Wendy said, waving toward the couch across from where the other women sat.

"*Looking at them together, I have to admit, you have good taste,*" I said.

"*Could we not talk about them, please,*" Levi grumbled in my head.

"*Sorry.*" Not sorry.

"Now Grace, what questions do you have about our activities?" Wendy asked.

"When did you decide to create this band of witches?" I asked.

"Coven," Kady corrected.

"Sorry. Coven," I amended.

"When I saw the need," Wendy answered. It was a general answer. Not what I was looking for.

"Fine. The night of the battle who was the third witch?" I asked. "Did any of you get a good look at her?"

Kady looked at Riley who looked like someone ran over her cat. She cleared her voice and spoke. "She looked like me," she said.

"What?" I asked, thinking I didn't hear her right.

"It was me. She looked like me," Riley huffed.

"I suspect it was a spell to make her look like Riley," Wendy offered.

"That's possible," Levi spoke up. "I've seen a spell which mimics someone else. A mimic glamour. Doppelgänger."

"*Where did you find that?*" I asked.

"*In Mable's book. I've been reading it,*" he said.

"*You and your books,*" I smirked. He grinned. They watched us during the exchange. We needed to become less obvious with our communication.

"We still don't know who it is," I stated.

"We will figure it out," Finley said.

"Yes, I want to know what all she did in town with my face on," Riley added.

"She came into my house with my children and approached Levi," I said.

"Why would she do that?" Riley asked.

"Pretending to be you," I replied.

"I would never compromise the integrity of your home. Especially with your children there. Besides, since we got back from Summer, I've stayed out of the way. I lived with Jenny until she moved out, and now Finley is staying with me. Believe it or not, Grace, I'm on your side," she said, which didn't surprise me about my brother. I figured he was shacked up somewhere. As for her claim that she was on my side, I knew Riley. The only side she was on was her own.

"So, this look-alike came into my home through my wards?" I asked, looking back to Levi.

"I opened the door, but I didn't invite her in," he said quickly.

"She crossed the ward without permission. I ordered her to report information back to me, and she had to comply. We've got to find a way to use that," I said.

"Information?" Kady wondered.

"Yes, she came to the house to tell Levi something about the ORCs because he had been to see you asking about them," I said.

"He didn't come to me but did call. He was acting strangely. He said that he'd seen me at the diner and that I needed to watch myself," Riley said.

"It wasn't you at the diner. It was her," Levi said, realizing his mistake in the first part of the day. Twice he was duped by a doppelgänger, and I had a pretty good clue as to who it was.

"She clearly has a hard-on for you," I said. "With both of *them* sitting here, that leaves only one candidate."

"Huh? Who?" Finley asked.

"Lisette," Kady and Riley said in unison.

"All the ex-girlfriends!" I exclaimed.

"No. Please to all that is righteous and holy! Please, tell me no," Levi groaned. Finley started laughing but shut it down after an evil look from Levi which invoked the bros before hoes rule.

"You are in the wrong RV if you are looking for righteous and holy, Levi," Wendy teased.

"For real!" I replied.

"It's not Lisette," he said, shaking his head. The strands of hair hanging down on his forehead swept back and forth. I'd decided with just that small movement that I liked the longer hair look on him.

"Denial looks bad on ya, Levi," I teased.

"Nothing looks bad on him," Kady said.

"Too true," Riley added.

"I agree," I said. *"Looks even better with nothing on, but if I said that out loud, they would probably agree."*

"I've got to get out of here," he said as he started to slide off the seat toward the door. I reached across, grabbing his hand.

"Stay. I'll stop," I promised.

"They won't," he whined in my head.

"Chicken shit," I said. He eased back in the seat, but wouldn't let go of my hand. I deserved that I suppose. We might as well be uncomfortable together.

"Who is Lisette?" Wendy asked.

"Levi's ex-ex-ex-girlfriend," Kady provided.

"She is a Creole voodoo priestess that we ran out of here last year," I said. "It makes sense that they recruited her."

"Swamp witch," Wendy muttered.

"But when?" Finley asked. "If they recruited her before Levi came to Shady Grove, then they knew more about your Father's plans for you long before we realized. Perhaps Lisette luring Levi to the bayou was part of their plan to keep him from coming here."

"Dylan said that Jeremiah had mentioned me to Nestor, and they had a disagreement about it. Dylan, of course, didn't want me here," Levi said. Thinking back to the words I'd read in Dylan's story, I knew Levi was right and that the ORCs had been in play for a lot longer than I had noticed. We were so focused on Stephanie and Brockton that they had slipped past us. Slicker than shit on linoleum. One thing was for sure, they were doing everything they could do to separate me from Levi Rearden. Thankfully, they hadn't, and they wouldn't. Not ever.

CHAPTER SEVEN

Tabitha stared at me across the table. "Something is different about you today," she said.

"No, not really," I replied.

"I think so," she said as she waved to Nestor to bring her another drink.

"Where is Remy?" I asked.

"Working on some houses. He said Levi has helped him out a lot," she replied.

"He has, but I'd rather him be home a little more often," I said.

"Oh, so, you are ready to admit that you love Levi Rearden?" she teased.

"No," I said flatly. "But he's family, and now he's the only adult in that house with me. I need to keep my sanity."

"Aydan is progressing very well. Now that he's talking, I suspect he won't shut up," she laughed.

"He's hilarious, actually. I love them both to death, but I need adults," I said.

"Tough thing to find in this town," she said, looking across the room.

I turned to see who was back behind me. I thought I'd seen everyone that had come into the room, but I hadn't noticed Dominick there with a few of the other wolves from Troy's pack.

"Good grief," I moaned. "Please tell me he's staying on that side of the room."

"He is. He cuts his eyes this way, but he won't come over here," she said.

"How do you know?" I replied.

"Because I'm pretty sure he doesn't want to tangle with Levi," she said.

I knew that if he talked to me again or tried to ask me out, Levi wouldn't be able to hold back no matter what his new position in town had become. However, if that is what it took to keep Dominick away from me, then so be it.

She watched the men on the other side of the room as they played pool and joked around.

"That crew gets loud sometimes," Nestor said setting a drink in front of Tabitha. "But they are harmless."

"Who is the dark-haired one?" Tabitha asked.

"Huh?" I turned back to find dark eyes staring back at me. He took two steps toward me, and Dominick put his hand on the man's arm. He jerked it away, approaching us despite the warning. I turned back to Tabitha and rolled my eyes. She giggled but hid it behind her hand as he sat down next to me.

"Hi," he said. Now that he was closer, I could see his darkened skin, not by the sun but by heritage. His black eyes twinkled in the darkness of the bar. "I'm Atohi."

"Hello, I'm Grace. This is Tabitha," I said.

"Nice to meet you, Grace. I'm part of Troy's pack, but I guess you know that" he said. "I promise I'm not here to bother you. I just wanted to introduce myself. If there is anything I can ever do for you, please feel free to ask. You protect us here in this city, and I'm willing to do my part."

"Do you work with the police?" I asked.

"I do, but there isn't much to police around here," he said.

"Hey man, come on," Dominick said from the front door.

"Go ahead. I'll catch up," Atohi called back to the other wolf. Dominick only met my eyes for a moment, then slipped out the door of Hot Tin.

"I appreciate your offer, but I'm sure that all my needs are met," I said. I hadn't decided if this was his angle or if he was genuinely trying to pay some sort of homage to me. The fact that Levi hadn't shown up yet, probably meant that I didn't feel threatened or uncomfortable around him. "May I ask what your name means?"

"Atohi is Cherokee for the woods. I love the outdoors, and my father foresaw that when I was born," he said.

"Perhaps he ensured that you would love it so that your name would mean something," I offered.

He smiled widely and replied, "Perhaps. I never thought of it that way, but it fits me."

"Cherokee," I said.

"Yes," he nodded.

"My fiancé was of the First People," I said.

"I knew of the Thunderbird. I hate that I never met him. From what I've heard, he was a great man," he said. "And now your son carries that tradition."

"Yes," I replied, thinking about how Remy promised to summon up some of the First People to bless my little thunder clapper.

"I wish you well, Queen. Nice to meet you, Doctor," he said as he stood. He made a slight bow to me. "If you would excuse me, I need to catch up with the guys."

"Of course, thank you for your generous offer," I replied.

He made his way to the door but never looked back. Once the door shut, Tabitha let out a long sigh.

"What?" I asked.

"If I wasn't involved, I'd take a dose of tall, dark, and wolfy," Tabitha said.

I laughed, "I'm telling Remy."

"Nah. I'll keep ol' Silver Tongue," she said.

"Now that is a fitting name for him," I said.

"You should know," she smiled.

"Oh, I do," I replied. "Do you think the wolf was working an angle?" He still struck me as suspicious. Troy had sung high praises for Dominick, but he had never mentioned Atohi. I made a mental note to ask him about the dark wolf in our next meeting.

"Grace, if he was, I couldn't tell. You attract all sorts of men though. Who knows?" she said.

I ignored her jab about attracting men. Other than Dylan and Levi, I had always attracted the wrong men. Well, except maybe Remy. He was a good guy. We just met at the wrong time. It made me happy to see him with Tabitha. They seemed very happy together.

"We should meet and chat more often. I miss this," she said.

"I agree. More adult conversation please," I said. We talked for another hour before Levi showed up to drive me home. I told him about the dark wolf, and he said he hadn't met him. I knew that tone of voice though. Levi would make a point to meet him since the wolf had approached me.

CHAPTER EIGHT

Winnie groaned as she looked at the paper on the dining room table. "Why is math so stupid?" she asked.

"You used to love math," I said.

"Not anymore," she replied.

"Besides math isn't stupid," I said.

"Yes, it is," she insisted.

Levi was sitting next to her trying to help, but she was in full "I don't want to" mode.

"If we work on this and get it done, I'll take you to the diner for a milkshake," Levi offered. Her face brightened as she nodded vehemently. I rolled my eyes and pretended that he hadn't just bribed my child into doing her homework.

"*It was the only incentive I could think of,*" he said.

"*It's okay. I just don't want to make that the habit,*" I replied.

"*Thanks, Mom,*" he said.

"I am *not* your mother," I said. Winnie giggled. She was catching on to us as well.

"*Yeah, incest isn't my thing,*" Levi said. I almost choked on the orange soda I was drinking. He grinned watching me flounder.

"*You may have not been taught this in Texas, but incest requires sexual contact,*" I explained.

"*So future sexual contact doesn't count?*" he asked.

I glared at him for a moment, then responded. "*In your dreams, Dublin.*"

"*No, that would be the past,*" he replied. Before I could think of a reply, he asked, "You and Aydan going to the diner with us?"

"Ice cream!" Aydan exclaimed.

"I guess that answers that question. Your Uncle Levi is spoiling you, Little Bird," I said.

"But it's yummy to my tummy," he smiled.

"Yes, it is," I conceded.

"Aydan, you look just like your daddy," Betty exclaimed as we came in the door. The pang of sorrow faded quickly as I looked at my child. Instead of allowing Betty's comment to distract me, I focused on how much she was right.

"He does look so much like Dylan," I said with a smile. I had moved forward from my grief to a point where my heart still missed my fiancé but being thankful for what I had had taken the place of that pain.

"Acts like him, too," Levi said.

"How so?" I asked as we took stools at the counter.

"All that thundering around," Levi grinned. Dylan definitely had his moments, and Aydan was using his thunderclap more often.

"I wanna see him do it," Betty said.

"No!" I replied.

Aydan who sat in my lap looked up to me when I raised my voice. He watched me closely. The thunderclap only came when I was upset. He knew a genuine upset from a fake one. I hadn't been able to provoke him by pretending to be mad. In fact, if I pretended to be mad, he would just laugh at me. Little Stinker.

A group of young men entered the diner making their way to the other stools. Part of Troy's pack. Atohi and Dominick were with them. A smaller man entered after them. He moved toward them but flicked his eyes to me. I saw fear in them.

"You see that?" I asked Levi who rarely missed a thing.

"Yep," he replied as he ordered a strawberry milkshake for Winnie.

"What about you, Grace?" Betty asked as I watched the wolves interact.

"Um, nothing for me, but a small bowl of ice cream for Aydan," I said.

"Ice cream!" Aydan exclaimed. Betty laughed at him.

"Your daddy liked ice cream too!" she said.

"Who doesn't?" Levi asked.

"Weird people," Winnie answered.

Betty hustled off to take orders from the pack. The smaller man stood behind everyone. He didn't seem like he was going to order anything when Atohi called back to him.

"Runt, get up here and get some food in you," he said.

"Okay," he replied timidly.

"That's rude," I said.

"Unless there is trouble, you should let Troy handle it," Levi said.

I had agreed to stay out of pack business unless it interfered with Shady Grove's stability. Troy and Amanda kept a tight rein on the shifters in town. Since October, we had added a few more panthers and a family of snapping turtles. They kept to themselves for the most part. The wolves had grown in number as well. Several litters had been born, and the size of the pack had grown to almost fifty. Amanda kept me updated on new arrivals and births. She and Troy seemed to be managing it quite well. Troy had made

Dominick his Beta, but watching him with this group, I questioned that decision.

The wolves were loud and boisterous, except for the little one. He ended up getting the tail end of most of the jokes. I felt bad for him, but I could also see the look in Levi's eye, urging me to stay out of it. Dominick didn't instigate the jokes for the small guy, but he certainly laughed at them. He made eye contact with me a couple of times. For those moments, I didn't see the humor in them. But it wasn't shame either. I couldn't figure the former Alpha out.

Of this group, though, Atohi was clearly the most outspoken.

"Eat up, Runt. We have fights tonight," he said. The other wolves laughed.

"*They have fights on Friday nights. I've seen them. It's pretty brutal, but Troy says it helps with aggression,*" Levi said.

"*That small one will get obliterated by those bigger guys,*" I said.

"*Don't discount a small wolf. They can be fast and nimble. I'm willing to bet Callum will give them a run for their money,*" Levi said.

"*Callum,*" I repeated. "*You know him?*"

"*Yep. He's young, but a good kid,*" he said.

"*Levi, you are all of 25 years old,*" I said.

"*I am 26 thank you very much,*" he grinned.

"*Same difference,*" I said. "*What's your middle name?*"

The devil grinned but didn't answer.

The ruckus across the room got louder as they continued to tease Callum. Once Betty brought out their food, the noise lessened, but not by much. They were extremely polite to her, thanking her for refilling their drinks, but when it came to the smaller wolf, they were relentless.

I wanted to bound out of my seat and defend him. He took it

all in stride, never showing weakness to them. I may not understand pack politics, but I knew what bullying was.

"We need to go before I lose it," I hissed to Levi.

"Yeah, sure," he responded. "Can I get a to-go lid for Winnie's
milkshake?"

"Sure thing, honey," Betty responded to Levi.

I hoisted up Aydan, but Levi quickly took him from me. He
grabbed my arm in the process because my attention was on the pack.

"Leave it, Grace," he urged.

I huffed but marched outside to drown out the noise and frustration. The late fall night called to me. A still quiet. A light
breeze. Dark figures emerging from the shadows.

"Levi!" I said.

He was behind me in an instant with Aydan on his hip. He'd
left Winnie inside.

"Here take him," he said, handing my child back to me.

"Momma!" Aydan said, pointing at the men emerging from the
shadows of the trees. I didn't have time to count as I walked back
into the diner.

"Give him to me," Betty said, reaching across the counter. I
handed him over as they ducked down.

"We've got your back, Queen," Dominick said.

As I returned to Levi, I found him standing in the parking lot
holding Excalibur. The sword brightened the darkness. The
wolves filed out around us to face the men crossing the street.
They were dark-skinned and wore feathers in their hair. Most of
them were dressed plainly in jeans and flannel shirts. They were
most certainly Native American.

"Did you feel them cross the ward?" I asked Levi in a low tone.

"I felt something move, but it was so fast that I didn't detect it
as human," he replied.

"My Queen, if I may?" Atohi said, striding up next to me.

Levi and I turned our gaze to him. "What is it?" I asked.

"They are First People. I will speak to them if you wish," he said.

"Are you sure?" I asked.

"I do not fear them. Nor should you," he said.

"Alright. Go ahead," I said.

Atohi walked out in front of us with his hands outstretched at his waist. He spoke to them in a language that I didn't know. I felt a presence close to my shoulder. I cut my eyes to the side, realizing Dominick had moved closer to me. Levi still stood in front of me. He showed more maturity than I expected, not taking his eyes off the approaching men. I felt his intensity through our bond. I also felt the power that rushed to him as he held my father's sword.

After speaking for a moment with the men, Atohi turned to us.

"They are here to bless your child," he said. "The Thunderbird."

Levi lowered the sword. We had been waiting months for them to show up to bless Aydan and his abilities. To accept him as Dylan's son and heir. I didn't know specifically what we had to do, but I was thankful that Atohi was there to translate. I felt a warm hand glide up the inside of my arm.

"Careful with him, Grace. He isn't what he seems to be," Dominick muttered.

"Get your hand off her," Levi spoke softly through gritted teeth. The warmth of his hand disappeared. I didn't dare look to indicate that I missed it, but his touch was heated. I pushed the sensation to the back of my mind. Levi took two steps back, putting himself between Dominick and me.

"Sorry, but you should know that he isn't a good person," Dominick said, then walked away calling the wolves to him as he left.

Atohi looked over his shoulder to Dominick and nodded.

Dominick returned the gesture, and the wolves shifted, bounding off into the darkness. Atohi walked back over to us.

"On my honor, these are the men that the Star Man called to bless your child," he said.

"I'll call Remy," Levi said as he stared off in the direction of the departing wolves.

"Levi," I said softly.

"I'm fine," he muttered as he pulled out his phone.

"Levi," I repeated. He put his hand on my shoulder turning slightly to look down at me as his phone dialed in his other hand. I leaned over putting my cheek on his hand.

"*I contained it for as long as I could. I'm sorry. I'll get better,*" he responded.

"*Don't let him touch me again,*" I said.

His eyes darted to mine as the slick twang of Remington Blake murmured through his phone.

"Hey, Remy, we've got some of your people down here at the diner," Levi said, searching my eyes.

"*He was warm,*" I admitted.

"Yeah, see you in a minute," he said, hanging up the phone. He wrapped his arms around me and squeezed. "It will get better, and he didn't mean anything by it."

"You are defending him now?" I asked.

"I just know how much I'm attracted to you, and it's difficult to hold back. He and I are in the same position," he said.

I moved back out of his arms. "No, you aren't. You are my best friend. You live in my house."

"Which might make it worse," he said.

"Oh," I replied.

A portal opened to our left, and Astor stepped through with his sword. He looked at the visitors then back to us.

"It's all good, Duracell," Levi said.

Astor's ginger hair jutted out in a wild, disheveled manner. It was unlike him to look so unkempt. Then it hit me. The man *was* a newlywed.

"Astor, you look well-rode," I said. Levi snickered. I'd seen Astor blush, but his face, neck and hands turned a deep red.

"Are my skills needed?" he muttered.

"No, we are fine," I replied.

"Very well," he said, swinging his sword in a circle to open the portal again.

"Looks good on you," I called to him. He looked back to me and winked. The portal swished shut behind him.

"Lucky bastard," Levi said.

"Indeed," Atohi echoed. I hadn't realized he was still paying attention to our conversation.

"Thank you for your assistance, Atohi," I said.

"Of course, my Queen. I am at your service." He bowed at his waist then returned to the visitors.

Remy pulled up in a Lincoln Town Car. He and Tabitha exited the vehicle. She approached me while Remy joined Atohi. They shook hands as if they knew each other.

"They friends?" I asked Tabitha.

"Remy knows most of the First People. Just part of his association with them. Atohi is a midnight Cherokee wolf. Have you seen him shifted?" she asked.

"No," I replied.

"He's completely black. No other color on him. His coloring is rare," she said.

"Troy used to be almost black, but I've noticed his color lighten," I said.

"He takes on the characteristics of his pack as the alpha. Kind of like representing them all," she said.

"It's a good thing I don't do that," I said.

"I dunno. You might look cool with Luther's fire wings," Levi interjected.

"That would be awesome," I admitted. "Dominick says that Atohi isn't a good person."

"I dunno. I've talked to him a few times when I've patched the wolves up after their fights," she said. "He seems okay. It's not like we know Dominick that well either."

"True," I responded.

"Plus, we know Dominick has an agenda," Levi said.

Tabitha smiled. I knew she was about to tease him. I could see the look in her eyes. "What agenda might that be, Levi?"

"Grace. His agenda is Grace," Levi said flatly, trying not to play her game.

"He moving in on your girl?" she pressed.

"No," Levi responded.

"It takes more to rile him up than it used to," she said to me.

"Not really," I said. "He's riled up on the inside."

Levi rolled his eyes, then turned his attention to the conversation going on with the visitors. He wasn't very good at pretending not to listen to them.

But then, Tabitha threw him a bone, "It's not like Levi has anything to worry about though, right?" She decided to turn her efforts to make one of us uncomfortable to me. It worked.

"Absolutely nothing," I replied.

"See, Levi. Nothing to worry about," she said. Levi only grunted in response.

Remy approached us with Atohi and the men following him.

"Grace Ann Bryant, Queen of the Exiles, Daughter of Oberon, I present to you Chaytan of the Sioux, Hosa of the Arapaho, and Talako of the Choctaw. They have come to meet the new Thunderbird and bless him," Remy said.

"I would like to represent the Cherokee in this matter," Atohi said. "If these men and you approve." He nodded toward me.

"The midnight wolf is welcome to represent his tribe. Is that acceptable to you?" Chaytan asked me.

"Yes, of course," I replied. "Welcome to Shady Grove. I offer to meet whatever needs you have while here and am happy to present to you my son."

"Keme Rowtag was a good man, and his passing is a loss for this world. My condolences," Hosa said.

"Thank you," I replied, trying to maintain control of my emotions. "Levi, would you mind getting Aydan?"

"Be right back," he said.

"Ask Luther to come with us and bring Winnie," I said. He nodded, then ran back into the diner.

Remy had explained the blessing ritual to me. I dreaded it because we had to return to the place that Dylan died. In most cases that was impossible, but apparently, the traditional ceremony would take place where the Thunderbird died or at an erected memorial.

"I understand the Phoenix is now your daughter," Chaytan said.

"Yes, Wynonna, my adopted daughter is now the Phoenix. She is being trained by our friend, Luther, who is Ifrit," I said.

"Ifrit!" Hosa exclaimed. "Is he safe?"

I smiled. "He is a kind and gentle man unless provoked. I suggest you stay away from his mate. She's the banshee inside the diner there," I said.

"We had heard your kingdom was diverse. This is a good environment for the Thunderbird to grow up in. His skills are perfect for this situation," Hosa said.

"Yes. Dylan was perfect here as well. Everyone loved him," I said.

Levi came outside, holding Aydan who looked at the men standing around me. His little eyes widened and he reached for me. Winnie and Luther came out of the diner behind them. Betty followed them out last. I took Aydan from Levi.

"Momma," he said, holding on to my neck tightly.

"He does not look like us," Chaytan said.

"No, he looks like his father," Hosa replied. "Who I believe could shift to look more like us."

"Yes, he could," I replied. Even though I had only seen it once, Dylan in his Native form was sexy as hell.

"Would you please place the child on the ground? We have to be sure he is the Thunderbird," Chaytan requested.

"Aydan, these men are here to meet you. Be Momma's brave boy and stand up for them," I said, bending at the knees to set him down. He stood up on his chubby legs, watching me closely. "It's okay, Little Bird. Momma is right here." I turned him around to face the men who watched the exchange closely.

Chaytan lifted his hands to the sky. Hosa, the silent Talako, and Atohi mimicked his movements.

"Great Spirit, reveal the truth to us this day. Is this the son of Keme Rowtag, the last of the Thunderbirds?" Chaytan called to the sky. Clouds billowed out of nothing forming a thick cover over the night sky. Chaytan lowered his hands, then clapped them together loudly. The other three did so with him in unison.

I felt power moving around us like I'd only felt once when Dylan shifted. Aydan took one step toward the men with his eyes fixed on the sky. His chubby arms reached out in front of him, and he slapped his hands together in the same way that they had. A crack of thunder erupted across the clouds with tendrils of lightning rippling over it. Winnie whimpered and Levi bent down to hug her. Luther and Betty stared at the sky in wonder as the lightning continued to ripple over the clouds.

"Wow," Tabitha muttered.

"Well, done, Aydan. We shall bless you, making you one of us," Chaytan said. "Please take us to the place where his father died."

"I don't want to go," Winnie cried.

"Winnie, do you want to stay here with Luther and Betty?" I asked.

"Yes, Momma. I can't go there," she said as a tear rolled down her cheek. My heart broke for her. I didn't want to go there either, but for Aydan's sake, I would.

"Do you mind?" I said, looking up at Luther.

"Of course not. She may stay with us," he said.

"I'll have her train as a junior waitress," Betty smiled.

"Alright," I said. Levi released her, and she ran to the door of the diner with Betty and Luther.

After watching her disappear into the diner, Remy spoke. "We have several vehicles here. We should be able to transport everyone to where Dylan died."

"I've got it," Levi said, shifting Excalibur in his hands. He stepped away from the group, pulling power as he passed me. Sweeping the sword in a circle, a glittering portal appeared before him. The field where Dylan died lied just beyond the portal. He stepped to the side, leaving the portal open for us to all walk through. It was amusing that he did it when Tennyson wasn't present.

Remy and Tabitha led our visitors through as I scooped up Aydan. Stopping beside Levi before stepping through I smiled at him. "Been working on it?" I asked.

"Yes, it was important to get it right. I'm still unsure about stepping into the Otherworld, but I will do it when the time comes," he said.

"Pretty," Aydan said reaching for the glowing edges of the circle.

"Yes, very pretty. Your Uncle Levi makes good circles," I said.

"Are you okay with this?" he asked.

"Dunno," I replied truthfully.

"No worries. I'm here," he said.

I stepped through the portal with Aydan into the darkened

field. The gypsy's RVs were in the distance. I was sure they probably saw us step through the portal. I didn't know if we needed to have an audience or not. I didn't know if it mattered. Levi closed the portal behind us. I felt his hand on my waist as we walked toward the gathering.

Chaytan reached out his hands over the place where Dylan died. I swallowed down my grief which bubbled to the surface.

"The memory of him is still here. He imprinted this place for his son," he said.

"What do you mean?" I asked.

"When one of our people dies, they leave behind a memory of their life. A soul imprint. Some call it a Chindi. Either way, part of Keme Rowtag is still here," he said. "Please place your child here. No harm will come to him."

"Can you explain to me what is going to happen?" I asked.

"Of course, as a mother, I'm sure you want to make sure he is safe. This is Aydan's inheritance. His father left behind a piece of himself that can only be taken on by his son. Our blessing of your son accepts him into our culture and the imprint will move into his life force. Knowledge of his power and responsibilities to the human race will rest in his heart. Just as it did for Dylan when his father died," he said. "We will also give him his First People name. Dylan's father named him Serafino Taranis. His other name was given to him by his mother's people, Keme Rowtag. Likewise, your son will receive a name from his father's people."

"Dylan picked out Aydan's name," I said, then realized it was a bit disrespectful. "And I'm sure you will give him a wonderful name to go with it." Not that he needed another name, but tradition, you know.

"If you are ready, we will begin. Please remain outside the circle," Chaytan said.

"Yes, of course," I replied. In truth, I wondered if a mother was ever ready to have *something* done to their child. I didn't know how this would affect Aydan or what the outcome would be after it was done. Levi stood close feeling my uncertainty, but I felt it from him as well. His heart was invested in Aydan. He had been a part of Aydan's life from the moment he was born.

"Come with me, Aydan," Chaytan said, offering his hand to Aydan. He reached up, grabbing one of Chaytan's weathered fingers, and allowed the man to lead him to the exact spot where Dylan left this earth. I took a deep breath to compose myself.

The four men took a spot to form a circle around Aydan. Reaching out with my instincts, I felt the breeze slide slowly over my arm. Each hair bent to its force. A chill rippled down my spine as the power of the four men was drawn to them through the atmosphere. In many ways, the Druids and the First People worship and conduct ceremonies the same. Without a compass, I knew each man stood at one of the four directions. This principle was important to their culture.

Chaytan began to chant and sway. Aydan stood completely still watching the men as they gathered their voices to join the man at the North compass point. Louder they sang and the clouds boiled overhead.

One by one each of the men shifted into an animal form. Atohi became the Midnight Wolf. Chaytan exploded into a large hovering falcon. Talako also spread his arms wide becoming a giant golden eagle. Feathers flew once again as Hosa became a foreboding, black crow.

"Birdy," Aydan said, pointing at the men.

Lightning flashed across the sky illuminating the field. A silvery haze formed above Aydan's head then lowered itself over his body like putting a shirt on over your head. He giggled as it settled into him.

"Levi," Remy said next to us. As I focused on what was happening to my son. My body tensed leaning forward on my toes.

"Huh?" Levi said, mesmerized by the sight.

"Levi!" Remy said with more force.

"What?" Levi snapped toward him.

"Hold her back," he replied.

"What?" Levi and I said, turning toward him.

The flashes of electric current in the sky quickened, and the static built up around us. I felt uneasy and my hairs stood on end.

"Hold her back!" Remy shouted over the growing storm.

Levi tightened his grip on my waist, as we watched the lightning striking the ground around us. My motherly instinct fired, and I lunged toward Aydan.

"Aydan!" I screamed.

Levi wrenched back as I tried to get to my son. Aydan smiled at the flashing lights, but my heart pounded in fear.

"Let me go!" I screamed, struggling against Levi's grip. I clawed at his arm as he wrestled with me.

"He's fine. It's okay," Levi urged. I wasn't sure he believed it himself.

"Let. Me. Go!" The command came too late.

With a loud boom, we tumbled to the ground. The last thing I saw was a thick, glowing, white bolt strike my son in the middle of the field.

CHAPTER NINE

In a matter of seconds, my mind processed a million thoughts. Nearly half them were different ways to kill Levi for holding me in place when my son was in danger. The other half centered around the panic for Aydan. Was he alright? Was he hurt? Was the bolt of lightning part of the ritual? What would Dylan think of me if I let something happen to our son?

When the haze in my head cleared, I shoved Levi away from me. The field was filled with smoke and the pungent smell of burning flesh.

"Grace, wait," he begged.

"You better be glad I don't kill you on the spot!" I snarled, climbing to my feet.

"Remy said..."

"That's your excuse?" I yelled. Levi's eyes widened, realizing how serious I was about ending his life.

"Grace, Aydan is fine," Remy said as he helped Tabitha off the ground. The man could be lackadaisical in a four-alarm house fire.

"Fuck both of you," I said, rushing towards the mound of smoking flesh in the center of the men.

"That sounds like an excellent proposal," Remy quipped.

I ignored him as I ran to my son. Levi followed me but kept some space between us. He knew I wasn't joking. Never stand between a mother and her child.

"Aydan! Are you alright?" I screamed as the little human ball unfurled.

Long hairy legs, skinny arms, and a head full of sandy blonde hair emerged in the smoke. But steady cobalt eyes focused on me as he tried to stand up.

I stood in horror looking at the young man who had taken the place of my son. He looked old enough to drive. My hands covered my gaping mouth.

"I'm okay, Mom," he said. A wide grin formed on his face.

A smile I had dreamed about. A smile that I knew. A memory of his father.

"Aydan?" I whispered as I approached him slowly.

"Yeah, it's me. Can't you tell?" he asked, looking down at his new arms and legs.

"Where is my baby?" I said as my voice trembled. My hands shook as I reached for him.

The four men had reformed into their human shapes, wearing the same clothes as before. I realized then they were shifters like Dylan when he became Thunderbird.

"The Thunderbird must be more than a child, but not quite a man," Chaytan said.

"No," I whimpered. Levi moved closer, but he dared not touch me.

"His body had to change to accept the knowledge and power of his father. Had he taken it on as he was, he would have forgotten it as he aged slowly. He is still your son, and we must name him," he said.

"You have done quite enough," I fussed, staring at my teenage son.

"It's okay, Mom," Aydan huffed. "Don't go all crazy and stuff."

I started to scold him, but I just couldn't. I had just lost 3 or 4 years of his already accelerated life. What was I going to tell Winnie?

He walked toward me naked as a jaybird. Good grief. He was almost a man. He was a not so miniature Dylan.

"I just can't. This is. Oh, my goddess..." I stammered.

He looked me in the eye and placed his too large hand on my shoulder.

"I'll always be your baby boy, Mom," he said.

I stumbled toward him as the tears began to fall. His long, lean arms wrapped around me in a tight embrace.

"I'm too young to have a teenager," I muttered.

His laugh started low in his chest then rumbled out in full force. I heard Levi snickering behind me as well.

"*You and I will have words later,*" I said to Levi.

"*I know,*" he replied with no added argument. One thing about Levi was that once he dug a hole, he'd stand in it instead of digging it deeper.

"A fine-looking young man," Remy proclaimed.

"You knew this would happen?" I asked.

"Didn't you?" Remy asked.

"Obviously not," Tabitha said, smacking him on the arm.

"I just assumed Dylan would have told you about a Thunderbird's blessing," he said.

"When? When I was pregnant? He wasn't here. After he was born? He was not here!" I exclaimed in frustration.

"This is probably why you couldn't slow his growth," Tabitha added. She was trying to calm me down.

I looked at my son who now stood almost eye to eye with me.

"Really, Mom, I'm fine," he said.

"Well, I'm not!" I exclaimed.

Another presence moved into our conversation. Atohi cleared

his throat before he spoke. "Grace, if Aydan had reached maturity before he was blessed, then the Thunderbird tradition would have been lost forever. It's not only important to our people but for the whole world that he exists. We meant no harm. I am surprised that Dylan never told you our ways," he explained.

"Dylan did not associate with our people as much as other Thunderbirds in the past. We believed this to be because of his split heritage. We hope that your son will interact with us more than his father," Chaytan said. "Forgive me for not explaining it completely."

Aydan listened to them intently as he stood near me. He nodded his head silently as they spoke of his father as if he knew the things that Dylan had done.

"What else is there before you can go?" I asked, hoping to hurry them along. I needed space to wrap my head around this one.

"Just his name and I would like to give him a token of his heritage from our people," Chaytan said.

"Anything I need to know about that?" I pressed.

"No. It is a name given to me by the Great Spirit. It was weaved in the clouds by the Spider Woman in a dream I had," Chaytan said.

"What is it, Sir?" Aydan asked. At least he had manners.

"Our people shall call you Yas Shikoba. It is the Navajo word for snow with the Choctaw word for feather," Chaytan explained.

"Snow feather?" I asked.

Chaytan smiled widely. "Yes, watch," he said with a light in his eye. He retrieved a strand of beads from his pocket, offering it to Aydan.

"Thank you. What is it?" Aydan asked as he took the beads.

"These beads will teach you to shift," he said.

Ayden tied the strand of beads around his neck. He ran his fingers over the beads and smiled his father's dazzling smile.

"Mom, stand back," he warned.

Stepping away from him moved me closer to Levi who was a ball of knots. He pushed back his emotions as I neared. I'd let him stew a little longer. He needed to understand that our partnership was a priority but nothing was more important than my children.

Aydan bent his knees then leaped into the air. With his arms outstretched, they seemed to sprout feathers which quickly covered his whole body. Before gravity took over, he opened his beak and screeched in the darkness. When he took flight, the storm clouds dissipated as we watched an entirely white raptor soar across the sky.

"He has a little of his mother in him," Atohi said with appreciation.

"He's magnificent," Remy exclaimed.

Aydan circled high above us before dipping down toward the ground. His shifting back wasn't as smooth as his initial shift. He hit the ground half-bird and half-man, rolling to a stop.

"Gotta work on that landing," he laughed.

Levi took the opportunity to approach him. He had taken off the shirt that he was wearing. He offered Aydan a hand to pull him off the ground, then the shirt which Aydan pulled over his head. Levi's scars were open for everyone to see. As far as I knew, no one here had ever seen them. My eyes cut to Tabitha who looked at Levi then back to me. I just closed my eyes blocking out the reason why Levi had scars the in the first place. Aydan stood at least 6 inches shorter than Levi as they stood next to each other.

"Well done, Aydan," Levi said.

Aydan slapped him on the shoulder in a bizarre display of foreknowledge of man to man gestures. "Thanks, Uncle Levi. Mom, did you see?" he asked.

"I did. It was wonderful," I said as my mother's heart simultaneously ached with loss and pride. "Your father would be proud."

"You think?" he asked.

"Yes, Aydan, he would," I said with no doubt of it in my mind. Thankfully, I had taken pictures along the way to one day show Dylan how his son grew up. We continued to take them after Dylan's death. Levi had pushed me to do it because he said that's what parents do. I had those images to hold on to going forward. My baby was gone. Replaced by a nearly grown man.

"I wish I could have known him," Aydan said.

"Don't worry. He left some things for you," Levi said.

"He did?" Aydan asked.

"Yes, I wrote the story of how he met your mother. It's a good story, and when she thinks you are ready, you can read it," Levi said. "She's right. He would be very proud."

"Were you and he friends?" Aydan asked.

Levi laughed. "Most of the time."

"Cool. Then you can tell me what he was like," Aydan insisted.

"Everyone in town knew him. We will all tell you what he was like," Levi said.

"You okay, Mom?" he asked.

"Yes, Aydan, I'm okay. Just a little shocked," I said.

He walked over to me, then hugged me tightly. "I'm so glad I have you since he is gone," Aydan said.

"I'll always be here for you," I replied.

Atohi and Remy agreed to see that our visitors' needs were met. Levi and I used his home spell to go back to the house. He was on the phone with Luther, telling him what happened and asking them to keep Winnie for the night. We decided to introduce her to Aydan tomorrow.

As Levi talked, he gathered some clothes for Aydan to wear.

They were too big for him, but at least he had something to wear for now.

"Wow! So, I have a sister too," he said. "That's great!"

"You might not think so when she starts begging you to color with her," I said. It made me smile as he explored his world for the first time. A unique perspective on growing up. He and I sat in the living room for a long time talking about family and friends. I told him about Finley and Nestor. He was eager to meet them all. His tone of voice and enthusiasm for life reminded me so much of his father. I knew from the moment that Aydan was born that he was going to be more like Dylan than me, but I had no idea how much.

Levi joined our conversation but remained mostly quiet. I knew that our disagreement in the field still bothered him. I wouldn't get to rest until we talked about it. Neither would he.

Aydan yawned after a while, and Levi and I caught it too.

"I have a room here?" he asked.

"Of course, but I'm afraid the bed is too small," I said.

"He can have my room. Just let me grab a couple of things, and you can sleep in there," Levi said.

"Where will you go?" I asked.

"I'll sleep down here in Astor's old room," Levi said.

It made me suddenly sad to know that I would go to bed, and Levi wouldn't be in the next room. There was a comfort in knowing he was so close. But my son was now a teenager and needed the bigger bed. I watched Levi rush upstairs to get some things out of his room. He came back not long after with his old backpack. The sleeves of a couple of different shirts hung outside of it, along with one leg of a pair of shorts.

The clothes in his hands he offered to Aydan who grabbed the "Don't Mess with Texas" t-shirt and a pair of drawstring shorts. He replaced the bigger shirt Levi had given him earlier with the tee which looked like the one that Levi had when he moved here. I had to admit looking at them brought back memories and the realization that Levi had developed not only in power but in stature as well. More importantly, Levi wasn't the lost young man that moved into my trailer.

"Thanks, Uncle Levi," he said. Even his voice sounded like Dylan. Maybe an octave or two lower but it was uncanny. I wondered how much Dylan sounded and looked like his parents.

"No problem. You are welcome to anything that is up there until we can get you a few more things," Levi said. "I'm going to get settled in the other room. Get a shower."

"Okay," I replied. "Come on, Aydan. I'll show you the room."

"Okay," he said looking back to Levi, then to me.

Levi nodded then trotted off to the back bedroom on the lower floor.

As Aydan and I went up the stairs, he watched down the hallway where Levi disappeared.

"Hey, Mom," he asked.

"Hm?"

"Why doesn't he sleep with you?" he asked.

"What?" I said, turning around at the top of the steps.

"You and he seem close," he said.

"We are, but not like that," I said.

"Why not?" he asked.

"It's complicated," I replied.

"Because of Dad?" he asked.

"Partially. Your father hasn't been gone very long," I said, as I continued to walk to Levi's old room. When we went inside, Aydan asked so many questions. It made me uncomfortable, but I had to keep telling myself that this was my son. Anything he asked, he deserved to know. I wasn't sure what all he did know since he had the rapid growth. I'm not sure who was more confused, him or me.

"But you love Uncle Levi," he said.

"I do," I admitted.

"So, you just aren't together like that," he said.

I sat down on the bed with a sigh. "I miss your father. It pains me to think of replacing him. I haven't had time to process it all. It wouldn't be fair to Levi to make a move on my feelings when I still have so much emotion wrapped up with your father."

"I see. I think," he said. "But what if something happens to Levi?"

"If something happens to him, I will be devastated. It is all very complicated," I replied.

He sat down next to me. "This is weird, isn't it?"

"Yes, very," I replied.

"My instincts tell me that it's normal, but I see your face. You are sad," he said.

Apparently, he had his father's ability to read my every emotion.

"I loved being your mother. I loved watching you learn new things and grow. You were already growing faster than humans grow. We were trying to make the best of it. Now all of that is gone," I said.

"But you still love me?" he asked.

I nudged his knee with mine. "Of course. I will love you until the day I stop breathing," I said. "You and Winnie are my purpose for continuing on after I lost Dylan. Everything that I do, I do it to make a safer place for you and her."

"There are bad things out there," he said.

"Yes," I replied. "Levi and I do our best to protect you."

"I want to learn to fight as my father did," he said.

"How do you know he was a good fighter?" I asked.

"There are just some things I know," he replied. "It's like they put things in my head. I want to protect you. I want to protect my sister. I even want to learn to help Levi."

"Your father protected this whole town. He was the sheriff. He took very good care of us all," I said. "And in the end, he gave up his life to save Winnie."

"I would do the same thing," he said.

I looked into his cobalt eyes and said, "I want you to live. Grow up. See the world. I want you to stay out of this fight. I'm fine with you protecting your sister. I get that, but Aydan, this world needs you to live. You are the last Thunderbird. Until you have a child of your own, you will be the only one. I think we have to protect that."

He hung his head, but I lifted his chin. Kissing him on the cheek, I smiled at how wonderful it was to have him like this. A constant reminder of his father's undying love for his family. I forgot the regrets of not watching him grow up, and decided to be thankful for what I had. That was the thing that kept me going after Dylan died. It would continue to drive me forward to make the hard decisions. To push us to war. To take back what was ours.

CHAPTER TEN

After Aydan went to sleep, I went downstairs to grab a drink out of the fridge. Levi was waiting for me. I tried to ignore him, but he had not seen fit to put a shirt on. It was hard to ignore that. He stood in the darkness of the kitchen watching me cross the room. The moonlight from outside hit his hair showing droplets of water where he had taken a shower. When I opened the fridge to grab an orange soda, the light illuminated the room and his body. The glint of tears rolled down his cheeks.

"Levi?" I said, letting the door close. He wiped his cheeks with the back of his hand.

"Yeah?"

"What's wrong?" I asked.

"I stepped out of line. I shouldn't have held you back from Aydan. It was wrong of me, but all I could think about was keeping you safe," he said.

"If you hadn't, I might have been harmed," I said, trying to console him. My anger had waned after talking so long with Aydan. What happened to my son was completely natural for his being and power. I needed to get over myself in order to be the mother that he needed during this transition. Which meant, I needed to forgive Levi for following his instincts to protect me. His natural reaction to the situation.

"You aren't mad?" he asked.

"I want you to know that if it ever happens again, I don't know if I can hold back from hurting you to get to my children. I don't want to ever have to make that choice," I said. "You lose in that decision every time."

"I know that. You are absolutely right," he said. "You are upset though."

"My child is almost a man," I choked out.

"I know. Just a few hours ago I was chasing him around the room," he said. "I had plans for us. I wanted to take him fishing, teach him to ride a horse, and teach him to play guitar."

"I'm pretty sure you can still do that," I said.

"Yeah, but I like chasing him around the room," he sighed. "Like a father figure. Hell. Now I'm like his slightly older brother."

"Not nearly as cool," I said.

"Not nearly." He paused, thinking over his next words. "But that's nothing compared to what's going on inside of you."

My lip trembled. "Just like Dylan, I have to be thankful for what I have. He will be able to protect himself better now. He said he wants to learn to fight."

"I can teach him," he said.

"I don't want him to fight! He's my baby!" I protested.

Levi reached for me. I started to resist, but I needed comfort. I needed him. I laid my head on his chest and wrapped my arms around his waist. He stroked my back lightly.

"I'm sorry," he whispered.

"It's not your fault," I replied.

"No, I'm really sorry about holding you back. You are my number one priority and protecting him is just as important as protecting you.

I lost sight of that for a moment. Not to mention, the thoughts that went through your head on wanting to kill me scared me just a little. When I realized what Remy was saying. I just reacted," he said.

"Remy is a bad influence," I muttered.

"That was an excuse. Not a very good one either," he said.

"Thanks for not letting me get melted by a lightning bolt," I replied, stepping away from his embrace.

He didn't say anything for a few minutes while I sipped on my orange drink. When I sat it on the counter to go to bed, I felt his desire for me to stay with him for a little while longer. So, I lingered.

"You stayed up there with him for a while," he said.

"He had lots of questions about our family," I said. "It's like he knows life, but not his life."

"Like what?" Levi pressed.

I leaned back to look at him in the darkness. "Were you listening in?" I asked.

A shit-eating grin crossed his face and he laughed nervously. "Honestly, no. But I know when you are beating around the bush," he said. "Spill."

"He asked why we weren't sleeping together," I said, too emotionally drained to put up a good fight.

His face lit up. "Oh, really? I like the new older Aydan. He's my new wingman."

"Shut your pie hole. He's not anyone's wingman," I said.

"Yep. I'm gonna start calling him Goose," he teased. "Wait. What did you tell him?"

"I said that it was complicated," I replied.

"It's really not. Here. Repeat after me. Levi, come to bed with me," he laughed. I glared at him and he laughed louder. "Getting you riled up is too much fun."

"Well, I hope that keeps you warm at night," I smirked.

"Being in bed with you wouldn't, Little Miss Ice Queen," he said as he continued to laugh.

I turned on him to stomp off. "I'm gonna..." I started to say as he jerked me back to him leaning into my ear from behind.

"Tell me what you are going to do to me," he growled.

I shivered, then realized I was completely turned on by that. He let go quickly as I jerked away.

"Whoa!" he said. His shocked look morphed into pure predatory mode. I put my hands up to keep him away as I walked backward.

"Levi," I said.

His grin lifted on one side of his mouth more than the other. Every move he made toward me was slow and deliberate.

"You can run, but there was no mistaking *that*," he said as his voice dropped an octave.

"I've never denied being attracted to you," I said in my defense.

He moved closer as I continued to move toward the steps.

"*That* was more than just attraction," he said, lowering his chin. "*That* turned you on."

"Levi, stop. I mean it," I said, trying to sound convincing. This wasn't the right time. This wasn't it. My emotions weren't ready no matter how much my body betrayed me.

"Shame on you, Grace, for wanting a man barely older than your son," he continued his stalk.

"I swear! Levi!" When he was overt like this, I could barely contain the flip-flopping fairy inside of me. She was itching to get some action. Any kind of action. I told her to sit down and shut up.

Just before I bounded up the stairs away from him, he grabbed me again. This time he pressed his hand into the small of my back pulling me back to his bare chest which I was hyper-aware of now.

"If you had wanted to get away, you could have just skipped upstairs," he said as his face hovered above mine. In my panic, I hadn't thought of that. He kissed me once along my jaw. "I'm gonna let you go because you aren't ready. I feel that. I feel all of it."

I swallowed. "Okay." It came out in a whisper.

He released me, stepping back to give me room. A part of me wanted what he was offering. The other part screamed in protest. Time to run.

"Goodnight, Levi," I muttered.

"Goodnight, Gloriana," he said. Something in his tone seemed almost familiar. Comforting. Like he should have been calling me by that name all along. I convinced myself that he had just gotten my emotions all twisted up. Dismissing it, I climbed the stairs, not trusting myself to look back.

CHAPTER ELEVEN

Aydan got up just as the sun rose, and I went downstairs to make breakfast. I didn't know what he liked, and neither did he. So, I made a big breakfast. As the bacon fried in the pan, Levi appeared, shirtless still. He punched the button on the coffee pot to start it up. I had forgotten to do it. He leaned over the counter, taking a peek at me. The shit-eating grin hadn't gone away either.

"Shut up," I said.

"I didn't say anything," he laughed. "Morning, Aydan."

"Hey, Uncle Levi. Mom is making breakfast," he said.

"Duh! I see that, Goose," Levi teased.

Aydan laughed. "Goose?"

"Oh, yes. I've got a movie that we are going to watch together. You will love it!" Levi said, taking a seat at the bar in the kitchen. Aydan sat on the stool next to him. I kept my back to them. I wasn't sure I'd be able to focus if Levi continued.

"Great! Mom called my grandfather. He's coming to see me, but I really want to meet my sister," he said.

"Grace, want me to go get Winnie?" Levi asked.

"Maybe after breakfast. I talked to Luther this morning. They aren't opening the diner today. She's fine with them for a little bit. I called Finley too, but he didn't answer. I want them to see first. Maybe they can be here when we bring Winnie home," I said.

"Sounds good," Levi said.

"Mom, why did you adopt Winnie when her mother died?" Aydan asked.

"Um. Well, her mother, Bethany, had me listed as her legal guardian," I said.

"But her last name is Riggs like mine," he said.

"Yes, your father adopted her. It's what made her his official daughter so that she could receive his Phoenix powers," I explained.

"That and your mom made her a full-fledged fairy," Levi added.

"How does that work?" Aydan asked.

"It's not complicated, but a royal fairy has to do it with approval from Summer and Winter," I said.

"So, she became a winter fairy first, then Phoenix?" he asked.

"She was technically dead when I gave her the ingredients to become a fairy," I said. "Our hope was that it would make her body morph into a supernatural vessel to contain your Father's fire."

"It's really cool. I can't wait to see what she can do," he said. "But she won't know me."

"She's smarter than her age. I bet she will," I said. I hoped she would. I hoped this didn't set her training back. She loved being the big sister even though we told her that Aydan would outgrow her.

Rufus began to bark to let us know that someone was pulling up. His doggie hearing had its own supernatural qualities. He'd kept his distance from Aydan. His wet nose twitched in the air as he smelled the young man that had taken my baby's place, but he wouldn't get near him. The fact was in his bird form, Aydan could easily carry off a little wiener dog. Rufus would be a good snack. I'm sure Rufus' instincts were to stay away from the predator much like he did when Troy was around.

"Hush, Rufus. All that racket. I declare," I said. "I'm going out to talk to him before he comes in."

"Alright. We will be right here," Levi said as he scooped up Rufus. It seemed to quell the dog's anxiety.

Nestor pulled up outside in his old beat-up pick-up truck. Ever since Mable got out of our holding cell, I've stayed in contact with him constantly. I knew she wasn't below using him to hurt me. He was tired. I could see it around the edges of his eyes and the slump of his shoulders.

"You okay?" I asked.

"I'm fine. What's wrong with Aydan?" he asked. I hadn't told him everything on the phone. I just wanted him to get here so that I could show him. It was hard to say that my toddler was now a teen.

"You don't look fine," I said.

"Gee, thanks," he said trying to smile. He relented after I glared at him. "The wolves have been in Hot Tin every night. Late. I've just not gotten enough sleep."

"You need help. We can find someone to work with you," I said. "I'm sure we could."

"Grace, what is wrong with my great-grandson," he pressed, ignoring me. Sometimes I wondered if I didn't get my stubbornness from him.

"Do you know anything about Native American blessings? The kind they give to their supernatural beings?" I asked.

"No," he replied.

"Well, some men showed up last night to bless Aydan. They took him out to the spot where Dylan died. They said a part of Dylan was still there. The part which was the full power and knowledge of a Thunderbird. It was Aydan's inheritance. They blessed him, and that power settled on Aydan," I said.

"And?" he prompted.

"And the inheritance couldn't be placed in a child. So, they made him a young man," I said.

"They what! Did you know?" he blurted out.

"No. Remy thought I knew what it entailed, but Dylan didn't talk about the Thunderbird heritage much," I said.

"Is he okay?" Nestor asked.

"He seems fine like it was a completely natural occurrence. He knows how things work, but he's learning who we are. He's anxious to meet you," I said, as we approached the front door. Just before I opened it, I warned him. "By the way, he looks just like his father."

"What?" he said, as we stepped inside. Aydan jumped to his feet in anticipation.

"Hello!" Aydan said enthusiastically.

I nudged Nestor who stood with his mouth hanging open. "Um, hello, Aydan," he said.

"I know it's a shock, but I'm so excited to meet you," Aydan said, smiling that radiant smile.

Nestor walked toward him slowly taking in the change in Aydan. Levi sat silently in the recliner. Thankfully, he had decided to put on a shirt. He nodded his head toward the chair.

"No, that's fine. You sit there. I can sit over here," I told him, as I made my way to the other chair in the room. I picked up a throw pillow to sit down in it.

"I wasn't offering the chair. I was offering my lap," he grinned.

I threw the pillow at him, and he died laughing. Now I knew why they were called throw pillows. I looked back to Aydan and Nestor who had just finished a big hug.

"Aydan, your Uncle Levi likes to talk in your mother's head. I assume he said something inappropriate," Nestor said. He'd seen us talk through the mental bond enough to know exactly what we were doing.

"You can do that?" Aydan asked.

"Yes. Levi and I share a blood oath. We, unfortunately, are very connected," I said.

"Unfortunately? Actually, it sounds pretty cool," Aydan said.

"Thanks. I think so," Levi said with a smile.

"It's fine until he starts saying rude things," I said.

"Then you throw a pillow at him," Aydan surmised.

"Or whatever else is handy," I said.

"And he loves every minute of it," Nestor added.

"I do!" Levi admitted.

I rolled my eyes and decided to ignore him. Rufus stirred at my feet with a small growl, then we heard footsteps on the porch. Finley was here.

He let himself inside before I could stop and warn him. Aydan turned from the couch to see him enter. He stood again to greet my brother.

"What in the Otherworld is that?" Finley asked. He knew who it was without me introducing him.

"A fully blessed Thunderbird," I said.

"Damn, Aydan. You look just like your father," Finley said moving closer to Aydan.

"Everyone says that," Aydan replied. "Your hair is cool."

"Thank you," Finley said beaming with pride.

"It's great if you want to look like a she-elf. Legolas would hit that," Levi teased.

I snorted as Finley's blue eyes flared with anger toward Levi. Aydan thought it was hilarious.

"Wait a minute. Do you know who Legolas is?" I asked.

"Yeah, sure. Lord of the Rings," he replied.

"How do you know that?" I asked.

"It's in my head," he said. "Lots of things are in my head. Like when Levi called me Goose. There is a reference there that I can't place."

Finley smirked, "You called him Goose? He's your wingman now?"

"Yep. He thinks I should be sleeping with Grace," Levi said. Aydan blushed.

"Levi!" I exclaimed.

Finley and Nestor laughed. "Well, I see he has good sense," Finley said, rounding the couch to hug Aydan. "I'm your Uncle Finley, and I don't need a wingman."

Levi coughed. "Sloppy seconds."

"Enough!" I growled.

Aydan looked confused, and Nestor hid his face. I knew he was laughing.

"Don't blame me that you gave up a good thing," Finley said.

"I raised my ambitions," Levi said with a wink to me. As if I didn't know he was talking about me.

"New subject, please," I pleaded. "Aydan has lots of questions."

"I do. Who is Riley?" Aydan said.

I slammed my palm on my forehead.

"She's my girlfriend," Finley said. "She used to be Levi's girlfriend."

"Oh, you stole her from him," Aydan said.

"No, I broke up with her," Levi said.

"And I've been gently picking up the pieces of her crushed heart," Finley said.

I groaned behind my hand.

"Oh, I get it now. Sloppy seconds," Aydan said. "Man, I've got a lot to learn."

I groaned again for effect.

"Levi, please go get Winnie," I said.

"She isn't here?" Finley asked.

"No, we wanted to break it to her with you and Nestor here for support. If you can stay," I said.

"Sure," Finley nodded. "I've got to teach my nephew about women."

"No, you don't," I said.

"Yes, I need to know about women," Aydan said.

"You may decide you like men better," I said.

Aydan cocked his head sideways, then shook it. "Nope. I'm pretty sure I like women. I mean, I haven't seen any, but I'm thinking women. Especially if they look like you, Mom."

"No one looks like your mother," Levi said, as he walked over to me. He leaned down over me, then kissed me on the cheek. "Be back soon."

What the hell was that? I stared at him as he grabbed his jacket from the closet, then stepped outside. I heard a portal open, and I felt his presence move away from us toward town.

"Wow," Finley said. "What's gotten into him?"

"I dunno," I said.

"He's tired of waiting," Nestor said.

"Waiting on what?" Aydan asked.

"Your mother," Finley said, taking Levi's place in the recliner.

"Please. I'm begging you not to talk about me and Levi," I said.

Finley let it go, and Nestor started up a conversation with Aydan about Native American rituals. He wanted to know what Aydan remembered from the blessing ceremony.

"Well, I felt very small, but then I saw a sparkling dust swirl around me. The next thing I knew, I had long legs and arms among other things," Aydan said.

"What other things?" Finley asked.

I shot him a look.

"Like other parts of me grew too," Aydan said.

"Oh! That thing!" Finley laughed.

Aydan continued without understanding Finley's amusement.

"I knew my mother's face, and Levi was familiar. Both of you seem familiar too. I know the basics of life. Mom fixed breakfast this morning, and I knew she was cooking bacon," he said.

"Bacon is a given. Everyone knows from birth what bacon is," Nestor explained.

"Oh, okay," Aydan said, missing the joke.

"Do you know schooling? Like history and math?" Finley asked.

"I suppose. I know numbers, additions, subtraction, and that kind of thing," Aydan explained. "I know a lot of Native American history and the stories of our people."

"That's amazing," Nestor said. I sighed. "You okay, Grace?"

"Just lamenting the loss of my pudgy little baby boy," I said.

"I told you, Mom. I'll always be your baby," he said.

The conversation continued as Finley and Nestor got to know the new and improved Aydan. I continued to ache knowing he would never be a baby again. He was still my son. That much was obvious with his sandy brown hair and cobalt blue eyes. However, it wouldn't be long, and he would be a man. It all happened too quickly.

CHAPTER TWELVE

I met Levi and Winnie outside when they arrived. Winnie ran up to give me a hug. She squeezed tightly.

"Momma, Uncle Levi says Aydan is different. What did they do to my brother? Do I need to burn them?" she asked.

"No, little wildfire. Calm down. He's just grown up a lot faster than we thought he would," I said.

"He's bigger than me already," she groaned. I knew the feeling.

"Yes, he's nearly a man," I said.

"Will he know me?" she asked.

"He already knows he has a sister, and he can't wait to see you again," I said.

"I don't know," she said.

"What do you mean? You don't want to see your brother?" I asked.

"How big is he?" she asked.

"He's a teenager. Like the big kids at school," I said.

"I don't like the big kids," she said.

"This will be different. He's your brother. He can protect you from the big kids now," I said.

"What if I don't like him?" she asked.

"You will like him," Levi said. "He's pretty cool."

I held out my hand to her. She placed hers in mine. The warmth of her father's power rushed over me in a familiar sensation. It felt good to remember. The ache was still there, but at least now my focus was where it should be.

When we walked inside, Aydan waited for us behind the couch. Winnie let go of my hand and clutched my leg. Aydan looked confused.

"Give her a minute," I said. He nodded, but he looked like his heart would break if she didn't respond to him. "Winnie, this is your brother, Aydan. Go say hello."

"He looks like daddy," she said.

"That's because he is Dylan's son," I said.

"Hi, Winnie," Aydan said. He squatted down so he would be eye level with her. "It's good to meet you."

"We've met," she said.

"Yeah, but I don't remember it," he explained.

"Oh," she said. "I think I liked you better as a baby."

My first instinct was to correct her, but I decided to let it play out.

"I think Mom thinks the same thing," Aydan said with a smile.

"Whatever. I love you no matter what," I said.

"Do you?" Winnie said, looking up at me.

"Of course. You and Aydan are my children. I love you no matter what kind of craziness happens," I said, stroking her sweet face with my hand.

Bramble and Briar decided this was the perfect time to appear. They landed on the back of the couch looking at Aydan.

"Oh, he's nice," Briar said.

Bramble elbowed her. "Down, Kitty," he said.

"Hi, I'm Briar," she said offering a small hand to Aydan. He offered her a finger, and she shook it. "This is my..."

"Mate. I'm Bramble," he said, shaking Aydan's finger. "We are Winnie's protectors. If you are mean to her, like big brothers can be, you will deal with us." The small guy's threat amused Aydan.

"Sure. Whatever you say. I wouldn't want to make you angry," he scoffed.

"That's right. You never know when a brownie is going to pee in your shoes," Bramble said.

"Ew," Winnie exclaimed. "You better not pee in my brother's shoes." She stepped forward with her hands on her hips.

Bramble bowed to Winnie, "As you wish, Princess."

"You are a princess?" Aydan asked her.

"I am. My mother is a queen. So, I'm a princess," she said.

"Guess that makes me a prince," Aydan said. The truth was, it did. He more than her. My blood ran through his veins. Winnie had some winter in her, but her father's abilities over-shadowed it. I wasn't sure she would ever be able to use any winter abilities. However, with his white feathers, I was sure my son would.

"It does," I said.

Winnie approached him cautiously. She reached up to touch his cheek. "You don't feel like Daddy," she said.

"I'm not warm like him. You got that power," he said. "But we both can fly."

"I'm not too good at that," she said.

"I'll teach you," he replied.

Levi moved closer to me, wrapping his arm around my waist as I watched my children discover some common ground. No matter how many times he touched me, the tingle that it sent through me shook me to my bones. There was a new feeling there though. I'd always run from Levi's advances, but I was suddenly filled with a dark gloom. A warning. I stepped away from him out of instinct.

"*What's wrong?*" he asked, sensing it from me.

"*I dunno. It felt weird,*" I said.

"*I've always touched you. It's never felt weird before, has it?*" he asked.

"No. *This was different,*" I said.

"I think that's a great idea," Winnie said. Aydan held his arms open, and Winnie walked inside of them to receive her hug. At least that was one less thing I had to worry about. The rest of the town would know about Aydan soon enough.

However, Levi looked at me. I saw hurt in his eyes. I was confused. He was right. I'd never felt like him touching me was wrong. I'd only refused to feel anything. Now with my guard down, alarm bells deep within me rang out. As if something inside of me was telling me to stay far away from Levi, which made no sense at all considering how close we were.

"*I'm sorry,*" he said.

"*It's fine. Just a strange sensation,*" I said.

"*If you'd let me touch you...*"

"No! *Don't go there,*" I said, grinning at his flirt.

"Yes, *ma'am,*" he said. Even in my head, I could hear that Texas accent.

CHAPTER THIRTEEN

The war council met at my house that evening. They were all happy to meet Aydan. Jenny gushed over him telling him how handsome he was. Aydan took all of it in with a smile on his face. He asked his thousand questions to everyone in the room until he was satisfied.

Troy and Amanda had wolf business to attend, so they weren't coming. Winnie convinced Aydan to go outside with her to the swings. Bramble, Briar, and Rufus went with them. I served sweet tea to everyone in the room. Astor brought his new wife Ella. They had the glow of newlyweds. I envied them in some ways. There was a time when I thought marriage was exactly what I wanted. Now, I wasn't sure it was possible. Not that Levi wasn't a worthy candidate, but that something inside of me suddenly felt repulsed by him.

His eyes met mine across the room. He wanted to talk about it, but we hadn't had time. We would. Just like the night before, if we didn't talk about it, neither of us would sleep. I refused to have something hanging between us that I might regret. He felt the same way.

"How are things between you and him?" Jenny asked, standing beside me in the kitchen.

"Good. Why?" I said.

"Just seems like you are giving into him a little more lately," she smiled.

"I was, but something has changed. It's not for the better either," I said.

"Like?"

"I can't explain it. It's weird," I said.

"Grace, I can understand recovering from grief. The shock of losing Dylan weighs on you, but it's not like Levi hasn't been here all along. Believe it or not, I saw that kiss in the parking lot of the Food Mart," she said with a devilish grin.

"How did you?" I asked.

"It was on the television. At the time, I said, damn, that boy can kiss. But I was wrong, that's a man over there," she said, nodding to him.

"*She's talking about me*," he said.

I rolled my eyes at him, and instead of grinning, he lowered his chin giving me that look.

"Hell, yes. I'd hit that," she said, watching him.

"Jenny!" I gasped.

"What? Just because I'm with Tennyson doesn't mean I can't admire a hot guy," she said. "Yep. I'd hit that into next week."

"I'd like you to keep your tentacles off of him," I said.

"Oh, see, you do care," she laughed.

"I do. Leave him alone," I restated for her benefit. She looked toward me to see if I was joking. She grinned when she saw my smile.

"Love doesn't always come only once in a lifetime," she said. "Trust me. I know this for a fact."

"You loved him? My father?" I asked.

"I did," she replied. "But I loved Lance, too. It was just unfortunate that both loves came at the same time."

"Come on, Grace. Let's get started," Levi said.

"He calls," Jenny prodded.

I gave her the middle finger salute. I hadn't done that in ages. Levi shook his head at me.

"*You are so royal sometimes,*" he said.

"*You are royal all the time. A royal pain in my ass,*" I said.

"*Kinky,*" he said.

I huffed then sat down on the couch next to Luther who cut his eyes at me.

"You okay, Grace?" he asked.

I flipped my hand toward Levi, and Luther chuckled.

"Let's get started, Levi. I have business to attend to tonight," Tennyson said in his gruff mob boss way.

"Sure. We are here to pick the timing for the raid into Oberon's castle to retrieve his helmet. Tennyson has suggestions for what time might be the best," Levi said by way of introduction. I used to lead these meetings, and still do when he isn't around. However, for the most part, King Levi took control.

"The fact is that I can't get a definitive location on the helm. We believe that it is located in the main ballroom, but the sources on the inside say that Brock has torn that room apart looking for it. Grace suggests that the helmet isn't in the ballroom. Our timing on the raid will depend upon a moment when there will be plenty of time to go in and get out if for some reason, we cannot locate it. Our friends within the Summer Realm say that Rhiannon is particularly pissed off at Brockton for the little disturbance to her fight with Grace and Astor earlier this year. She plans to infiltrate Winter to steal a few artifacts for herself. While some may consider it to be a bad idea to show up at the same time that she does, I think it's the perfect timing," Tennyson said.

"I agree," Levi added. "If we take a small group in, we might even go in unnoticed."

"Is she after the helmet as well?" I asked.

"I believe so," Tennyson said.

"I have no desire to cross paths with her after Marshall showed up at Astor's wedding," I said.

"Why is this helmet so important?" Luther asked.

"The wearer has sight beyond our fairy skills. It can see the wall between this world and that one. In battle, it allows the wearer to see the events before they happen," Astor said, adding foresight to what I already knew about the powers of the helmet.

"Why is it important to be able to see the wall?" Ella asked.

"If you can see it, you can destroy it," I said.

Ella gasped, covering her mouth with her hand. Astor wrapped a burly arm around her to comfort her.

"Brockton, as well as Rhiannon, seems to be hell-bent on tearing the veil apart allowing everything there to enter this world and vice versa," Tennyson said gravely.

"It would destroy both worlds," I said.

"They don't see it that way. They believe it will usher in a whole new era of rule for our kind. It's ambitious," Tennyson said.

"Sounds like you admire it," I commented.

"I said ambitious, but it is also foolish and deadly," Tennyson said.

"Our solution is to bring the helmet here to the vault. I've been researching some of the other artifacts that I believe Arthur had. I need to discuss it further with Grace to see what else would benefit us to grab while we are there," Levi said.

"Bookworm," I grunted which released the tension in the room.

"You should read more, Grace," Levi said.

"Why? You do plenty of it for both of us," I said.

"You should let him write your story," Tennyson said.

"Oh, hell no," I replied.

Levi grunted, "Why would I want to torture myself like that?"

"You love it," Ella interjected. I burst out laughing, watching the deep pink of embarrassment creep up Levi's neck to flush his cheeks.

"That's what all of you think," he grunted.

"No, we pretty much know it for a fact," Luther said.

"When is Summer making their move?" Levi asked, changing the focus.

Tennyson had to gather his composure to answer. "My source says that he can only give me a heads up when they start to make their move. We need to be ready to go at any minute. Grace, make sure you make preparations for your children. Perhaps you can get Nestor to start spending more time out here."

"I'm on call for that," Ella said.

"I will be here as well," Jenny added.

"Who all is going through to Winter?" Luther asked.

"Levi, Grace, Astor, Finley, you and myself," Tennyson said.

"You are going?" I asked. I knew Tennyson never made moves into Winter. He hadn't been to that realm in ages.

"Yes, I am. I will protect my King and Queen," he said. Jenny rubbed his shoulders which had straightened when he said it.

"It is dangerous for him to go," Jenny said.

"Jenny," Tennyson growled.

"It's dangerous for all of us. We are all exiles," I said.

"I'm not sure that I can even cross through the veil into Winter," Tennyson said. "But I'm going to try."

"No, you stay here. You can be the one to protect my children. Jenny can go with us," I said. "Or better yet, Troy can go with us."

"I will not let you die or him," he said in frustration. "I *must* be there."

Astor lowered his head refusing to look at him. I knew that Tennyson must feel some responsibility for my father's first death on earth. His affair with Jenny had split the kingdom. However, now was not the time for him to risk his life to step through the veil. I believed we had plenty of abilities among us to get in and out quickly without him.

"I'm going," he said firmly.

"Don't make me force you to stay," I said.

"Don't do that, Grace. I didn't bleed for you so that you could order me around," he grumbled.

"I didn't accept you so you could die for me without reason," I replied.

"Getting Winter back is the only thing that matters," he said.

"So, when the time comes to blow my Uncle into ice smithereens, then I hope you are there, but until then, I need you alive. We won't take that kind of chance. You stay here," I said.

"No," he growled. "I should have been here when he died. He stepped through to protect you. I should have been here. It wasn't how he wanted to do it."

"Do what?" I asked.

He stood jerking his suitcoat into place. Jenny reached out for his arm, but he jerked it from her.

"Lancelot," she purred.

He closed his eyes, grinding his teeth.

"You aren't leaving," she said.

"We aren't done," I added, but with a lower tone.

"I am done for now," he said.

"Please, my love, sit back down," Jenny coaxed.

We watched as her words sank into him. He shivered when she spoke. I looked through the spectrum to see if she had some sort of oath over him, but there was no magic involved. They were just so intertwined with each other that her words meant everything to him. His flashing aura calmed, and he sank back down into his seat.

"Forgive my outburst," he mumbled.

"I like a good outburst from time to time. Keeps things exciting," I said. His eyes flicked to mine, and I saw a bit of a twinkle there. From the moment I'd met Tennyson Schuyler, we had managed to have a couple of fiery arguments. Two very strong-willed people standing in the other's wake.

"Grace," Levi mumbled.

"Shhh, you. I've had enough of you tonight," I said with a wink.

"You haven't had nearly enough of me yet," he said.

My jaw dropped open, and I turned my head back to him.

"You've really got to start saying that stuff out loud," Jenny said. "I don't know what you say to her, but no one makes her flinch like you."

"Hush your mouth, Jenny," I hissed.

"Please tell me what you said," Jenny begged. The attention to Levi and me diffused the tension that had built up with Tennyson. I watched his eyes soften even more as she teased us.

"No," I warned.

He waggled his eyebrows. "I just told her that she hasn't had nearly enough of me yet," Levi said proudly. This caused everyone in the room to laugh.

"Levi Rearden," I fussed.

"Yes, ma'am?" he grinned.

"Shut your mouth," I said. I should have put some magic behind it, but I didn't.

"Yes, ma'am," he grinned.

Ella had managed to work herself into a fit of giggles. "I'm sorry, Grace."

"Whatever. He's a big talker," I said.

"Love talker," Astor corrected.

"That ain't love. That's arrogance," I said.

"Love can be arrogant," Tennyson said.

"You should know," Jenny teased.

"Meeting dismissed," I blurted.

"We aren't done, Grace," Levi said.

"Then get to it," I said in frustration. I couldn't believe he said *that* to these people. I was going to jerk a wart on him. And a knot in his tail. I might even find an ugly stick to beat him with, only that would be a waste of a pretty face.

"From this point, we are on standby to go. I will open the portal. Keep your weapons close and make arrangements for your families," Levi said, wrapping things up. "And Tennyson, I agree with Grace. You stay."

"What!" Tennyson boomed.

"We cannot lose you at this point. We won't take the chance," Levi said.

Tennyson's anger grew again. "The whole thing is taking a chance. If it's that dire, then Grace should stay too."

"Grace knows the castle," Levi replied.

"So, does Finley," Tennyson countered, pointing at my silent brother who had not taken part in the discussion at all. He sat on the stairs in the darkness listening to all of us. It reminded me of when we were children, and we would sneak around to listen to my father talking to his advisors and knights.

"Grace should be able to locate the helmet when none of the rest of us can. It is her inheritance," Levi added. "Plus, she will be with me. Nothing will happen to her."

I didn't know what to think about that statement. Levi had saved my ass more than once. He was a hero. Like Dylan.

I tried not to ponder on the thought for too long, but it occurred to me that Dylan saved my heart and my life. Levi had saved my life, and I refused to give him my heart. It didn't need saving. It needed mending. With each day that passed since Dylan's death, Levi had been doing that. Slowly and steadily. That was what had changed between us. I allowed myself to consider us. Not just as partners and best friends, but us, as a couple. I'd done it myself through giving him the sword which essentially made him the king to my queen. If I was the most powerful piece on the board, he was the most important. He watched me across the room with his sword between his legs. I'd never considered a recliner to be a throne, but he made it look like one with the confidence that seeped out of his pores.

Tennyson lowered his eyes. He knew Levi was right, and for some reason that I couldn't fathom, he let him be right.

"I will stay behind to keep Shady Grove and the children safe," he said. "Troy must go."

"I'll talk to him," Levi said. "Any other questions?"

"Did you meet with the witches?" Astor asked.

"We did," I said. "It seems that Wendy, Riley, and Kady are on our side, but I'm always wary of witches."

"I've known Kady for a long time, Grace. She wouldn't betray you now," Ella said. I didn't believe that, but I knew why she said it. They were friends and had lived in this town together since they were kids.

"Riley wants vengeance for her father. That is dangerous," Tennyson said.

"I agree. She's never been loyal to anyone but herself," I said.

"What about the witch that hunts her?" Tennyson asked.

I had almost forgotten that Jeremiah had said that Ceredwin hunted her. "I don't know anything about that situation," I admitted.

"I'll ask her," Jenny said. "She's more likely to tell me than you."

"Good. We need to know everything," I said.

"What about Wendy?" Astor asked.

"She's a wildcard, but I would expect that from a wanderer," I said. "She will do what fits her when it tickles her fancy. Just the impression that I get. However, I get the impression that the ORCs are an abomination to their practice. Their faith in their magic and how it is used will be a constant between them. I think they will help us to the extent that it damages the Red Cloaks."

"Anything else?" Levi asked.

No one answered.

"Thank you all for coming," I said.

After exchanging good-byes everyone left except for Finley who lingered in the living room waiting for everyone to leave. I knew he had more to say.

"Grace, would you see me out to my car?" Tennyson asked.

"Sure." I should have known he wasn't finished. He wanted to get the last word in. The old Grace wouldn't have allowed it, but the new Grace would.

Jenny walked out ahead of us. Stone opened the rear door of the car for her, and she sank into it. Stone closed the door and got into the driver's seat.

"I apologize for my outburst. However, I know you think this stems from your father's death. However, I want you to know it's more about him dying here in Shady Grove. When you moved here, he asked me to come here to keep an eye on you. I refused, focusing on my business and endeavors. I knew that Jenny would show up eventually too. I wasn't ready to face her either. However, I can't help but think that had I been here, we could have stopped Brockton. I admit there were times I had dealt with him on a business standpoint through his law offices. He was the devil you know. I never fathomed that he would make such a move on you. Or your father. I failed him again."

"I think you have more than made up for it by being here now," I said.

"I can never make up for it," he said.

"Tennyson, you are a valuable member of our team. We cannot do this without you. The empire you've built may have been for the wrong reasons, but it's helping us now for all the right ones," I said.

"The ends do not always justify the means," he said.

"No, but they soften the blow," I said.

"You are magnificent, Grace Ann Bryant," he said. "I never imagined you would develop any sense of humility. I watched you from afar, and you've grown into the Queen he expected you to be."

His words didn't surprise me. Tennyson was thorough and meticulous. Of course, he had kept tabs on me.

"It's this darn heart," I said, rubbing my tattoo. It twinkled with power.

He pointed a large finger into my sternum. "It's this darn heart," he said with a smile.

"Thank you, Lachlan," I said, using the name my father used for him.

He sighed. With a slight nod, he turned and opened the door for himself to join Jenny. I felt Levi, approaching from behind.

"If he touches you again, I'm gonna rip that tree trunk off and beat him with it," he said in a playful tone.

"Sounds gory," I said.

"Maybe," he said. "You okay?"

"Yeah. He's just lamenting his position with my father," I said.

"He's more than made up for it," Levi said.

"In his eyes, he could never make up for it," I said.

"That's what makes him a knight," Levi said.

I sighed. We had good knights. It was time to see what the white-haired one wanted.

CHAPTER FOURTEEN

"WHAT'S EATING YOU?" I ASKED AS WINNIE, AYDAN, THE Brownies, and Rufus came inside. Levi went into the kitchen to fulfill requests for beverages.

"Have you been out to the wolf fights?" he asked.

"No, have you?" I asked.

"Yes," he said. "They are interesting. Like an underground fight club."

"The first rule about fight club is no one talks about fight club," Levi said from the kitchen.

Finley and I stared at him for a minute.

"Huh?" Finley asked.

"I dunno," I replied.

"You know, he's really strange sometimes," Finley teased.

"Leave him alone. No one can tease him except me," I said.

"Yes, and you are teasing the hell out of him, aren't you?" Finley said.

"It's not like that," I said.

"Whatever you say, Glory," he said. "Anyway, the wolves. It's good exercise, but Tennyson is there most nights. Remy, too. They bet on the fights. It's just strange to me. I think you should go down there."

"Where is it at?" I asked.

"Where is what?" Levi asked.

"The wolf fight club," I replied.

"It's out past Troy's place," Levi replied.

"You've been there?" I asked.

"No. I just know it's there. I'm the mayor, remember?"

"By default," I replied. Finley snickered.

"What's going on out there?" Levi asked.

"You should go see for yourself. I'll stay and watch the kids," he said. "I need to get to know my nephew. He needs to learn a few manly things."

"Okay, she-elf," Levi said.

Finley wrinkled his face. Even with his alabaster skin in frustration was still beautiful. He couldn't help it. Bless his heart.

"I'm not leaving you here with my son," I said.

"You wound me, Glory. I love those kids," he said, holding his long fingers over his heart.

"Uh-huh," I mocked.

"I do. I'll be good. I promise," he said.

"Wanna go to a fight?" I asked Levi.

"It's a date," Levi said, as he took off up the stairs. "I gotta change clothes."

"It's not a date!" I hollered up to him.

"It could be a date," Finley suggested.

"Too soon," I said.

"Whatever, Grace. No one is going to question your love for Dylan if you start seeing Levi," he said.

"Since when have I cared what anyone else thought? It has nothing to do with that," I said.

"Go put on something nice," he said.

I looked down at my slouchy sweater and jeans. They were

nice enough. "I'm good," I said, as Levi bounded back down the steps. He wore khaki slacks and a deep blue button-up shirt. Only he hadn't quite got it buttoned up as he hit the bottom of the stairs.

"No, Levi looks nice, and you look like..."

"Tread lightly, Fin," I warned.

"Like a trailer park queen," he laughed.

I slapped him on the arm. "Fine," I huffed.

"You look okay, Grace," Levi said.

"You would say that if she wore a burlap sack," Finley said as the kids turned on the television.

"You don't even know what a burlap sack is," I said.

"Sure, I do. I heard someone say it at Nestor's the other night, and so, I googled it," he said.

"I rue the day you learned how to use a cell phone," I replied.

Reluctantly, I trudged upstairs to change clothes. I wasn't sure exactly why what I wore mattered. I could handle it two ways. I could either dress to the nines. Enough to put Levi in a tailspin. Or I could go one step above this and just look *nice*. Finley was right. Perhaps I enjoyed torturing Levi. I thought back to Dylan and how I had tortured him. He loved every minute of it. Levi did too, but I felt like his patience might run out. Something clicked inside of me. I didn't want his patience to run out. It felt too soon to move on. But I knew that in many ways loving Dylan was a risk. I didn't know how it would turn out. It turned out badly, but our love didn't. It was far more perfect than I imagined it could be.

On the other hand, loving Levi wasn't a risk. He had established himself as a leader with very little help on my part. It was like it suddenly awoke in him. From the moment he stepped out of the torture of the Otherworld, he had taken on more and more responsibilities. He grew up overnight. He still had a touch of immaturity with things, but I chalked that up to be his natural disposition. I loved seeing him brood.

"Hurry up!" Finley called up to me. I didn't know we were on a timeline. I stood in the middle of my room trying to decide. Middle ground wasn't a foreign concept to me. I decided that might be the way to go. If we were showing up to this as the leaders of this community, then perhaps I should look at it that way. A quick dig through my closet and I found a nice dress that resembled the red dress I wore the night that I got elected queen. Only this one was a light lavender color with a simple belt. I slipped into a pair of heels and took a look at myself in the mirror. I pulled my platinum blonde hair up into a ponytail. Sexy, but not. I could do this, but it wasn't a date.

"Well, damn," Finley said as I walked down the stairs.

"More like wow!" Levi said.

"I tried to go conservative," I pouted.

"You look great," Finley said. "Very queen-like." Which was exactly what I wanted. Levi just stared. He was like the dog on the cartoons that Winnie watched where his eyes bulged out and his tongue rolled across the ground.

"Are you ready?" I asked.

"Yes," he gulped.

"What is wrong with you?" I asked. He shook his head refusing to answer, but he offered his hand to me. I took it without hesitation. I had always taken it without thinking. Why did it matter now?

"Have fun," Finley said.

We walked out to the truck silently. He walked me to the passenger side to open the door for me. I watched him as he did it.

"Just get in," he huffed.

"Thank you, Levi," I said. His eyelids flared up in surprise. He knew I meant it. No sarcasm.

"You're welcome," he said.

We had driven through town before he began to speak again.

"It's been a while since you've not worn jeans or simple shirts. You look very nice," he finally admitted.

Since Dylan had died, I hadn't really cared about my appearance. Now I knew why he had that look. I had made an effort. In his mind, I had done it for him. He wasn't completely wrong. If my plans went forward, I knew if Levi was going to be the King to my Queen, that we might need to make it official at some point.

"I just needed time to get back in gear, but I knew I didn't have too much time before my responsibilities would catch up with me. Besides, I couldn't look like trailer trash with you dressed so nicely," I said.

"Grace, you have never looked like you belonged in a trailer," he said.

The rest of the ride was quiet. When we pulled up to Troy's property, there were cars parked up and down his long driveway. Stone and Bronx leaned on Tennyson's black land yacht but straightened up when they saw us. Bronx stamped out a cigarette, as Levi drove by them slowly. When we reached the house, he found a gap to tuck the truck into without blocking the drive.

I got out before he could help me. He scowled, but I grinned at him. He couldn't help but return it. Levi knew who and what I was. While it's nice for him to open doors for me, I'd rather do it myself for the sole purpose of aggravating him. Once again, his hand was offered, and I didn't refuse.

We made our way through a lighted path to the edge of the woods where two of the pack met us. Both looked uneasy as we approached.

"Grace, Levi, is Troy expecting you?" the one on the right asked.

"No," I replied.

"Maybe I should let him know you are here," he said while the other one remained silent.

"No, you will not," Levi said forcefully.

"Um, okay," he trembled.

"I'm not going to hurt you, Sammy, but we are here to observe the fights. That is all. No need to announce our presence. Are we unwelcome here?" Levi asked. His tone implied that the answer better not be anything other than what Sammy spewed out of his mouth without hesitation.

"Of course not. All are welcome to the fights," Sammy said. "Stay on the path. It will lead you to the fight."

Levi stepped forward, and I followed his pace. I expected to find a field where the wolves fought, but to my surprise, it was an actual octagon-shaped ring with netted sides. No one was in the ring as we walked up to the gathering. Bleachers surrounded the fight floor. The spectators weren't just the wolves. Along with Tennyson and Jenny, Remy and Tabitha, I saw many other citizens that I recognized. Troy saw us reach the edge of the crowd and rushed up to us.

I could sense the panic in him before he spoke.

"Grace, what are you doing here?" he asked.

"We came to watch the fights. Is that okay?" I asked.

"I didn't know you knew about the fights," he replied. He looked back over his shoulder making eye contact with Amanda who approached us.

"I don't know much about them which is why I am here," I explained. In part, it was true, but I also wanted him to know that I was somewhat disappointed that this whole thing wasn't mentioned to me at some point. To see at least two of my knights here, yet to know nothing about it bothered me. For so many years I didn't trust anyone. I'd given my trust to these people, and even though this might turn out to be no big deal, I thought that perhaps I'd been left out of this for a sinister purpose. I could never stop being paranoid about the people around me. I had too much to protect.

"We don't know why they didn't tell you about this or invite you. Let's just hear them out," Levi suggested. I wasn't sure when

he had become my voice of reason, but heavens knew I needed one.

"*Just too many secrets and betrayals in my lifetime,*" I said.

Looking through the crowd, my eyes landed on a man I didn't know, but it was clear that he was a cursed Unseelie fairy. He sat quietly on the first row. His stoic face and piercing eyes focused on me as if I should know him. His deep olive skin reminded me of my Uncle Brockton's glamour when he posed as a Greek lawyer. His defined cheekbones gave an edge to his face along with the neatly cut beard. Finally, I met his whiskey-colored eyes. In them, I saw fear, but I also saw defiance.

Tennyson bristled in his seat not far from the dark, but handsome man. The man slowly nodded his head to me, and inexplicably I nodded back to him. He never smiled or showed a hint of emotion other than the sternness in his eyes.

"Why don't you have a seat and watch?" Troy offered as he shooed away a couple of his guys that were seated ringside.

"Thank you," I responded with my eyes fixed on the man. He held my gaze. Levi guided me to the seat with a firm grip on my arm. Troy moved away from us to speak to Amanda.

"*Could you stop ogling that man? I know it's not a date, but geez,*" Levi complained.

I turned my head back to Levi breaking the attention of the dark man. A slight grin curled up on the edge of his mouth as he waited on me to berate him. I'd never known a man in all of my days that enjoyed me scolding him. "He seems familiar," I said trying to avoid giving Levi what he wanted.

"He should be," Levi replied.

"Who is he?" I asked.

"Tennyson says his name cannot be spoken here or in the Otherworld," Levi explained.

"No," I muttered, turning back to the man who had focused on the two men in the ring preparing to fight.

"What?" Levi asked.

"He wasn't just banished. He was forsaken," I said.

"Forsaken?"

"I was banished from the Otherworld, but the highest form of exile is called being forsaken. Those who suffer that punishment are executed and their names are forbidden to be spoken ever again," I said sadly.

"What is that?" Levi asked.

"What is what?"

"That look. The one you just made," he said.

"Nothing," I replied.

His hand slipped into mine, as my heart lurched. "Grace, it was something. I saw it for a moment. It was a deeper sadness than I have ever seen. Is being here with me making you upset? We can leave."

"It's not you, Levi. Just a painful memory. From long, long ago," I said.

"Would you share it with me? To ease that pain?" he asked.

"I can't. It was never to be spoken here or there," I said with a nod the man across the ring from us. His dark eyes flicked back to us, then away again.

Levi looked confused. "Is he someone you know?"

"That man looks familiar, but the one I speak of is different. Only a few ever suffered the path of the forsaken. They were men who were once loyal to my father, but he found falsehood or betrayal in them. Damning them to death. Erasing them from history," I said.

"Are you just remembering this?" he asked.

"No, but now that I see him, I realize that those who were forsaken are now living their second lives here in Shady Grove," I said. A flood of forgotten emotions rushed over me. I tried to reel them in as Troy walked to the center of the octagon. "I'm fine, Levi. I promise." However, I wasn't fine. Painful memories threatened to take over me. Levi didn't let go of my hand, so I leaned on him for support.

"*You know you can tell me anything. Whatever this is, I can feel the ache inside of you. It's as bad as when you think of Dylan,*" he said.

"*Yes, it is that bad,*" I replied.

Just before Troy began to talk, I looked up to Tennyson whose eyes were wide. His ears flinched as he swallowed. Tennyson would have been forsaken had my Father caught him in the Otherworld. I suddenly remembered why Lancelot never really died. He was due to die by the monarch's command for treason. The sentence had already been laid out, but no bounty hunter could ever capture him to bring him to my father. I realized now that Tennyson with his vast wealth and empire had probably paid each one of them more than what my father offered them, and he continued to live his life above while he was condemned below.

When I looked to Jenny, she tucked her arm inside of Tennyson's but looked down. She too had been forsaken. Only she had suffered the death that her lover had not. She returned to this world a grindylow, a cursed beast. My eyes floated back to the dark man. I wondered what sort of beast he has been cursed to be. I wondered what his name used to be, and what it was now. I could almost remember, but not clearly.

"Ladies and Gentlemen, fairies and shifters, welcome to fight night. We welcome our Queen to the gathering tonight and hope to provide her with a good show. I will relay the rules to anyone who does not know them. Two shifters fight like men. They are forbidden to shift. They must fight hand to hand with no weapons and no magic. There are no wards to prevent a shift or magic use. It must be a choice by the competitors to play fairly," Troy said as he turned in the ring. On each side, he wore a holster to bear the weapons I had given him, Driggs.

Another pang of emotion struck me. Levi squeezed my hand tighter, as I inhaled to compose myself.

"Our first fight is two newcomers to the ring. A couple of young ones who are eager to earn their places in the pack. Please give encouragement to Phelan and Ingo," he said as two young men bounced back and forth ready to fight.

Phelan stood almost six-foot-tall with dark brown hair and brown eyes. His legs were muscular with tight calves. He definitely had the weight and height on the other boy.

Ingo had a lighter brown hair the color of hay with pale blue eyes. His arms moved like lightning in front of him. While the other might out mass him, he definitely had the speed and agility that the bulk of the other man wouldn't allow.

"Ready?" Troy called. The crowd yelled to encourage the man they supported. The two young men nodded to Troy. "Fight!" he yelled, backing out of their way to allow them to fight.

CHAPTER FIFTEEN

PHELAN TOOK THE FIRST SWIPE AT INGO WHO QUICKLY dodged the strike to land a couple of punches as he moved. They landed just under Phelan's arm around his rib cage. Phelan growled in frustration. I feared we would see them shift before our eyes, breaking the rules.

"No matter how mad they get, they will not shift," a familiar voice said behind me.

"Dominick," I muttered.

"Good evening, Grace. Levi," he said politely. I couldn't see him, because he sat directly behind me. I was sure he wasn't sitting there when we sat down.

"Nick," Levi responded.

"Nick?" I asked.

Dominick chuckled behind me. "Yeah, my friends call me, Nick," he said.

"I didn't know you were friends," I muttered loud enough for both of them to hear above the cheers of the crowd as the two in the ring continued their dance.

"Sure, we are," Levi said tersely. Obviously not.

"Definitely," Nick added.

"Whatever," I responded. "Why won't they shift? I know it is against the rules, but can it be helped?"

"It's a teaching tool. If they shift, they are banished from the pack. It's about controlling the beast inside no matter how dire the circumstance. While the wolf is strong, you have to convince yourself that you are stronger than it," he explained.

"I see. Banishment seems rough," I said, knowing my own experience.

"We haven't had to do it. No one shifts," he said.

We watched the two men fight for a little while longer until the quicker opponent wore down the larger one. Ingo eventually won with a hard punch to a much slower Phelan, knocking him to the ground. Nothing seemed to be off or untoward here. I couldn't understand why Finley insisted that we come. I saw Tennyson and Remy exchanging money, but I wasn't appalled by it. If Troy thought it was fine, then I wasn't worried about it.

Stepping between them, Troy proclaimed Ingo to be the winner. The victor raised his hands over his head in celebration. The crowd cheered. The wolves were enthusiastic with their support. Dominick clapped lightly behind us. While the dark-eyed man across the way locked eyes with me again.

Suddenly the world swirled around me and my vision blurred.

"Grace!" Levi yelled. I felt his arms encircle me as I drifted into sleep.

Only it wasn't sleep, it was darkness. Echoing footsteps approached me. The dark-eyed man appeared in the shadows with his focus on me. He walked slowly toward me.

"Who are you?" I asked.

"Gloriana, don't you remember?" his deep, accented voice asked. Something middle eastern twinged along his English.

"No. You do seem familiar, but I cannot place it," I said. At first, he intimidated me, but now even in the darkness, he seemed kind.

"My name can be spoken here," he said.

"Where is here?" I asked.

"It is the place where the yazata walks," he said.

"Yazata. Angels? Are you an angel?" I asked.

"I am a soul, separated from my body, forbidden to return because of the curse your father laid upon me," he said. "The yazata allow me to walk here."

"Why am I here?" I asked.

"Time has a way of making even us old ones forget," he said.

"Couldn't you just tell me? I'm sure Levi is freaking out by now," I said.

He chuckled, "Then you don't know."

"Know what? I'm getting tired of this game," I said.

He took several more steps toward me. "Would it help if I did this? I can only do it here," he said, kneeling before me. He cut his palm with a curved knife. "I am Palamedes, Knight of the Round Table, servant to my King Arthur. As his daughter and heir, my blood is your blood. I swear my fealty to you."

"Your blood is my blood. I accept your service from this day forward," I replied mechanically.

I gasped as a flood of memories overwhelmed me. My life before banishment. My friends above before the council kicked me out. I choked trying to say his name. When you were forsaken, your name was stripped from you and from all of those who lived in the realm. His name had been ripped from my vocabulary. At this moment, I wanted to rebel against the compulsion to not speak it. However, no matter how much I forced it. It wouldn't come.

"My Queen. Do not stress yourself. In this life, I am known as Zahir," he said.

"I accept your oath as given, Zahir," I mumbled. "You chose Lancelot over my father."

"I would again and again. Your father's mind was poisoned by the very one who killed him. The one who killed him again. Gloriana, you are destined to break the cycle. I will breathe my last upon the sword that dares to bring you down. I will redeem myself," he said.

"There is nothing to redeem. My father was wrong," I said.

"Bold statement," he replied.

I nodded. It was. Growing up, I knew the story of Arthur, his queen, and Lancelot. So many of the written tales, including those that Taliesin recorded painted Lancelot badly, but Guinevere as a whore. Yet, from what I knew now, they only had eyes for each other, and my father didn't care until Mordred drove them all apart. Of course, when I read the stories, I was blind to the fact that my father Oberon was Arthur.

"I want to set right what once was wrong for all of you. For all of those in Shady Grove. Where were you when Rotsam was here?" I asked, knowing they were both of Persian descent.

He smiled with a large toothy grin. "I heard that you sent him out of here with nothing but his sword."

My face blushed at the terrible game that I had played with Rotsam Dastan. "Well, he really was a horse's ass."

"That's what made me decide to come here. I wasn't so sure about you, but I liked your style," he laughed. "That is something I could fight for."

"Really?"

"Yes, my Queen," he said.

"How did we not know you arrived? Levi feels everyone who walks past the barrier," I asked.

"I came through this land. Not through yours, which I believe may provide a heads-up to a weakness within your safety zone. Now that I am here, I will monitor this realm for you," he said. "It will be my sworn duty."

"Zahir, I am so glad you are here, but we must go back. I can feel his panic," I said.

"I will say one other thing before I return you to him. It is obvious that your memory has been tampered with if it took you so long to remember me. Ask yourself what else you have forgotten. Have you forgotten *him*?" he asked.

"I will never forget *him*. It is my curse," I said. I also could not speak his name. Zahir spoke of another man forsaken that I had known.

"Are you sure?" he asked.

Before I could pressure him, I opened my eyes to see a panicked Levi looming over me. His dark blue eyes bore into me. The light tunes of his guitar tattoo flowed around me. Tabitha stood beside me watching me closely.

"Grace," Levi muttered, placing his hand at my neck. His power flowed over me sending a chill through me.

"I'm fine," I said, pushing myself up off the ground. Someone braced me from behind. I turned my head to meet the concerned eyes of Dominick.

"What was it?" he asked.

I looked back to Levi, then over his shoulder to where Zahir had been sitting. Only, he wasn't there anymore. "The man across the ring needed to speak to me," I said, showing them my blood-stained hand.

Levi grabbed it to make sure it wasn't my blood. "Who was he?"

"His name is Zahir, and he was once an old friend," I said. "Where is Tennyson?"

Levi helped me up as I looked up to where Tennyson and Remy were seated. I raised the blood-stained hand to my father's first knight. He nodded solemnly. He knew Zahir had been here, but I wasn't so sure who all saw him here other than me.

"Let's get you home," Levi said.

"Are the fights over?" I asked.

Amanda spoke from nearby, "No, we still have the challenge fight."

"I want to stay," I said. Levi knew the look. We were staying, and there was nothing he could do to convince me otherwise. He sat back down, and I took my place beside him. "Carry on!" I encouraged Troy who stood on the stage looking down at me.

"We aren't going home until you tell me what happened," Levi said.

"You might have my father's sword and stand by my side, but one day, you will learn that you don't order me around, Levi Rearden," I said.

"And you will one day realize that anything I order you to do is for your own damn good," he said. My bard did have a backbone. Bravo. However, I meant what I said.

———

Troy walked around the ring drawing the attention of the crowd away from my episode. Most there would never know what happened to me, but I supposed I was good for a spell every once in a while. A spell was like a hissy fit, but instead of stomping and screaming, it involved fainting. Levi sat tensely, and I felt Dominick settle in behind me.

"For our final fight, we will have the challenge fight. Each week, we have this fight. The winner of last week's fight picks his opponent from any wolf or shifter that has stepped into the ring before. Currently, our champion for three weeks running is Atohi," Troy declared as the tall Cherokee man stepped into the ring. The crowd cheered his arrival.

While they cheered, I commented to Levi to try to ease the tension, "It seems a conflict of interest to have someone come into the ring that might challenge your leadership. If Troy has fought in the ring, what happens if someone challenges him?"

Levi started to speak, but Dominick leaned between us. Anger rolled over Levi's face like an asphalt packer. I squeezed his hand to calm him. "No one will challenge Troy or me. It's just the honor of the pack. If they challenge Troy, they would regret it. He's never lost."

"He's been challenged before?" I asked.

"Early on, yes. He had to establish his dominance. Being an alpha isn't enough. You have to prove it," he said.

"Have you been challenged?" I asked.

"I have," he replied.

"Have you ever lost?" I pressed.

He grinned, "I never lose."

Levi grunted, clearly proving to Dominick that he was losing the battle for me. But since the wedding, I hadn't felt the same vibe from Dominick. As if, he had changed his strategy somehow. I wasn't sure what he was up to, but it didn't seem like he was trying to catch my attention in that way even though Levi still felt threatened by him.

"Atohi, please pick your opponent," Troy said, waving over the crowd. Several of the wolves around us boasted that they could take him, but I had the feeling that Atohi was formidable in the ring. He paced around the fencing looking at the opponents in the crowd. When he reached where Levi and I sat, he nodded to us, then moved around the ring. He paused in front of a group of men who seemed to be the younger crowd in the pack. Atohi lifted his finger to point at the smallest one in the group, Callum.

"Callum Fannon, I challenge you to fight me in the ring," Atohi's strong voice boomed around the area. The crowd grew silent as the smaller young man stood.

"No, he is no match for him," I hissed. "I'm tired of this bullying."

"Grace, stay out of it," Levi said.

"You saw what he did to him in the diner," I said.

"He's right, Grace. You should stay out of it, but don't underestimate Callum. He's a good fighter," Dominick interjected.

"I accept," Callum's unsure voice answered the challenge.

"Can he refuse?" I asked.

"If he wants to be disgraced," Dominick said.

"This is hazing," I said, jerking my hand away from Levi.

"Grace," he grunted as I stood.

Callum walked past me as he made his way to the gate to the ring. "Callum," I said calling out his name. His back straightened as he turned to face me.

"My Queen," he said, dipping his head in respect.

"Don't do this," I said.

"I fight for my honor, my Queen," he said.

"At what cost?" I asked.

"At whatever cost," he answered nobly. His voice and demeanor sounded confident even though his body language told me different.

"I would intervene on your behalf," I said.

"I beg you not to. Instead, may I ask for your favor to win," he said.

He wanted me to bless him. To cheer for him as he stepped up to what was sure to be an easy win for Atohi. I stepped up to him, seeing the resolve in his eyes.

"Callum, may the goddess aid you in this fight so that you may emerge victorious," I said.

He sighed with a smile, "Thank you, my Queen." Dipping his head again, he turned away to enter the ring. Levi pulled me back to my seat, and I sat on the edge of it, hoping that by some miracle, Callum didn't end up hurt or worse.

CHAPTER SIXTEEN

Blood ran from Callum's nose where Atohi had landed several punches. I felt each one of them in my bones. From what Dominick said, there was no mercy rule. They fought until Callum either couldn't fight or reached a point where he felt like he could tap out honorably. He was still dodging punches and kicks by his opponent who was clearly on a different skill level.

"It seems dishonorable to choose an opponent for a for-sure win," I said.

"Callum has never lost, but he's never been in the challenges before. This is his chance to prove his level," Dominick said. "We heal up quickly. He will be fine."

"What is it about him, Grace? Why are you so concerned?" Levi asked.

"I dunno." I couldn't place it.

"Motherly instinct," Dominick supplied.

"Is it?" Levi asked.

"Maybe," I said. There was certainly a part of me that felt he was too young and weak. He needed protection. All of these people including Atohi were under my protection, but should they be? At the moment, I wasn't so sure as the crowd jeered and cheered each movement in the ring.

A cracking noise drew my attention back to the action as Callum hit the mat.

"Are you done, Runt?" Atohi jeered him. "I'm not even bleeding."

I growled as Levi slipped his arm behind my back. He leaned into my ear. "He will be fine, Grace."

"Let go of me," I said through my teeth.

"I won't, but I promise that I will intervene if I think it is necessary. Please trust me," he pleaded.

Callum gathered himself up, then lunged at Atohi hitting him quickly three times in the ribs. Atohi grabbed his ribs in pain, lowering his guard. Callum punched twice again at Atohi's face drawing blood before Atohi moved away. Now the younger wolves cheered for Callum, who seemed as though he could barely stand. Stumbling backward, I saw his face contort like he was fighting himself as well.

"*He's going to shift!*" I yelled in Levi's head.

Levi jumped to his feet. "Fight it, Callum! Fight!" he yelled.

Callum waved his head back and forth like he couldn't. Atohi laughed at the younger wolf struggling to fight back his creature. The skilled fighter lifted his finger in what seemed like a taunt, but I felt the magic move as it had the night Aydan was blessed. A different source. A native source.

"*Atohi is forcing him to shift!*" I yelled again.

"Stop the fight!" Levi yelled over the crowd. Troy's hands went to Driggs, as he turned to look at Levi shouting. I rushed toward the ring trying to pull power but felt blocked by the power that Atohi pulled.

Before any of us could get to Callum, his wolf form burst out of his body in the blink of an eye. A solid white wolf stood with snarling teeth. With a few quick steps, Callum pinned Atohi to the ground who placed his arm in front of his face only to encounter Callum's teeth.

"Stop!" Troy yelled at Callum, who rolled on his side in a whimper. Blood poured from Atohi's arm where Callum had dug his teeth into the skin of his arm. Troy leveled one gun at Callum who didn't move. I didn't think as my magic rushed back to me. I just skipped to the small white wolf blocking his body with mine.

"No!" I yelled as the fire grew in Troy eyes. I looked down the barrel of Dylan's old gun with pleading eyes. "Please don't. It would be a mistake."

"No one shifts!" Troy growled.

"He used magic," I said.

"Who?" Troy asked.

"Atohi," Levi said, running into the ring. I felt him pulling power as the Celtic knots on his shoulder began to glow.

Troy lifted the other half of Driggs and pointed it at Atohi. "Explain!"

"I only used it to protect myself. He was struggling with the shift. We all saw it," Atohi feigned innocence.

"No, he pulled power before that. My power was blocked," I said.

"Mine too," Levi confirmed. "And you better lower the gun you have pointed at Grace or you will deal with me."

Troy dropped the gun pointed at me but kept the other trained on Atohi. "You've got two seconds," he snarled.

"I need more than that. Please. I'm begging," Atohi said. His confidence waivered with Levi and I standing against him.

By now Amanda and Dominick had entered the ring. Amanda moved up behind Troy in a solid show of support. Dominick rushed to Callum, trying to coax him back to human form. I felt the whoosh of power as the boy shifted back.

"*Clear the arena,*" I told Levi.

"Alright, everyone. The fight is over. Time to move out," Levi instructed. Tabitha walked into the ring with Tennyson on her heels. He held his sword in his hand and stood in the doorway.

"May I look at his wound?" Tabitha asked.

"No. He will heal," Troy said, keeping his focus on Atohi.

"I'm so sorry. I'm so sorry," Callum whimpered behind me.

"I'll take Atohi to the house, but Callum shifted. It's the rules, Grace," Troy said.

"Then I vouch for him. He comes with me," I said.

"Grace," Levi warned.

"I mean it. I claim him," I said. "You kick him out. Then I'll make him something in my household. I don't care, but you aren't kicking him out of Shady Grove."

"If I'm not in the pack, I'm no one," Callum whined.

"You will be in *my* pack," I said.

"You promised not to interfere," Troy said.

"I'm only interfering on the behalf of an innocent man!" I said. "This is *my* town. I have trusted you with this pack. I get the need for these fights, but *this* is different. *He* cut off my power." I pointed to Atohi. "Do you understand the implications of that? Of cutting off Levi?"

"I get it!" Troy yelled back at me. "I deal with the shifters!"

"I'm pulling rank on this one," I said firmly.

"Fine. Take him. Callum, you are banished from the pack. You no longer are welcome here," Troy said. "It's the rules, Son. I'm sorry."

"Yes, sir," Callum replied. His fearful eyes locked on me, and I nodded. Dominick helped him stand, and I took his small hand in mine. I'd forgotten he was naked as a jaybird, but it didn't matter. He needed help.

Troy asked Tennyson to help him move Atohi to the house. Amanda and Tennyson followed Troy and the native to the house. Before Dominick walked off, I grabbed him by the shirt and pulled him to me.

"You make this right," I growled.

"I will. I promise, Grace. I felt the power move, too. I'll do what I can. I'll call you if I have any news of what they do to Atohi. Thank you for taking him in," he said, nodding toward Callum.

"You felt the power?" I asked.

He smiled slightly. "I'm only half wolf."

"You devil," I said.

He smiled wider, "Not devil. Just fairy."

"Same thing!" I said as his smile infected me. "How can I not see that?"

"The wolf is stronger," he said. "I've never met my mother. I was always wolf until I was banished."

"What?" I asked.

"Another story for another day," he said. "I'll talk to Troy. He will listen to me." He ran off up the hill after his Alpha.

"Well, wasn't that cute?" Levi smirked.

"Get over it," I said. "I'm not interested in Dominick, and we aren't talking about this now."

"I'm teasing you," Levi grinned.

"I'm not laughing," I said.

"But you should be," he countered. "I can't help it if you have a stick up your butt."

Callum laughed at Levi's attempts to diffuse my anger. He knew that in moments like this the darkness tried to take hold in my heart. He refused to let it happen.

"Levi!"

"It's true, Callum. You'll get used to it. I'll take you two to the house, then come back for the truck," he said, taking my other hand as I held Callum's. "Home."

CHAPTER SEVENTEEN

ONCE AGAIN, LEVI SACRIFICED HIS CLOTHES FOR ANOTHER young man. Even though he was a few years older than what Aydan appeared to be, Callum and he hit it off nicely. I watched as the two of them joked. Levi and I sipped coffee standing next to each other in the kitchen.

"What are you going to do with him?" Levi asked.

"I don't know. I just know I couldn't let him leave Shady Grove when he was cheated," I said.

"Always looking out for the little guy," Levi commented.

"Like you," I said.

"Exactly like that. You took me in when you shouldn't have," he said.

"Why not?" I asked.

"You had no idea how sexy I would be," he said, lifting an eyebrow.

"I will admit that I had no idea at first what having a changeling living in my house would be like, but the first time you walked through the trailer without a shirt, I knew I had made a mistake," I laughed.

"Mistake?" he pouted.

"Oh, please," I scoffed.

"Please what?" he teased.

"You make everything sexual now," I said as I started to feel uncomfortable.

"No, you just take it that way," he said, trying to convince me.

Before I could speak, I realized that the boys had gotten quiet. I looked up to a set of green eyes and a set of blue eyes staring at me. "What?"

"Nothing," Aydan said, then turned back to Callum. "See."

Callum nodded. I didn't want to know what he was talking about with the other boy.

"Letting me stay was a mistake," Levi reminded me of our conversation.

"Absolutely," I teased.

"That hurts me right here." He pointed to his chest. "And other places. That turn blue."

"Levi Rearden," I muttered.

"Truth hurts. Man, does it hurt," he continued.

"Would you stop?" I tried to hide my smile behind my coffee cup.

"You could make it stop," he insisted.

"I could make it worse," I added. He groaned, then sighed. "Where is he going to sleep?"

"In Astor's old bedroom," I said.

"Where am I going to sleep?" he asked lifting an eyebrow.

I sat my cup down on the counter and started to walk away from him. "I'll bring you a pillow for the couch."

"*One day you will change your mind,*" he said.

"*Get out of my head,*" I replied.

"*Head rhymes with bed. I think your subconscious is trying to tell you something,*" he insisted.

"*I think my conscious is telling me you deserve blue balls,*" I said. He died laughing. I wasn't sure why it was so funny, but he continued to laugh as I realized the boys were staring at us again.

"He talks in her head," Aydan explained.

"Oh, that's cool," Callum replied. "You must be very funny."

"She's hilarious," Levi supplied.

"Hush your mouth, Levi Rearden," I said. "Time for bed, Aydan." Winnie was already asleep when we got home. I'd have to find out tomorrow how much Finley corrupted my son. He rushed out once I appeared with Callum, telling me that he had to get home. Home. Home with Riley.

"Yes, ma'am. Where is Callum sleeping? He can have my bed," Aydan offered.

"No, he can sleep in Astor's old room," I said.

"Oh, Uncle Levi gets the couch," he laughed.

"Yep," I said with a smile.

"You are hilarious, Mom," Aydan said as he jumped up to give me a hug. I kissed him on the cheek and tried to imagine my chubby little baby boy. "I love you."

"I love you too," I replied. He bounded up the steps, disappearing into Levi's old room.

"I don't want to take someone's bed. I can sleep on the couch," Callum said.

"Nonsense. I'll take you back there," Levi said. "Come on."

Callum stood up, then walked to me. "Thank you, my Queen, for interceding for me."

"You are welcome, Callum. Tomorrow I want to talk about what happened. Okay?"

"Sure," he replied.

"Alright. Get some rest," I said. His bruises were already healing. The wounds had closed not long before we left Troy's house, but from the way he carried his shoulders, I knew he felt defeated. I would have to find something for him to do. I had taken in Levi and Astor. Callum was no different. I seemed to be a sucker for lost souls. Probably because I had been in the same place in my own life.

I sat on the couch waiting for Levi to come back. He reappeared with a pillow and a blanket from the room. He sat down next to me.

"Tell me," he said.

"Tell you what?" I asked.

"What made you so sad talking about the forsaken," he prompted. I hadn't forgotten, but I hoped that by some miracle he had. He hadn't. I took a deep breath and tried to psych myself up for a conversation that I had never had with anyone. Not even Dylan. Levi slid his hand into mine and squeezed. "If you can't, I can wait."

"Really?" I asked.

"Of course," he said. "Believe it or not. I know when to leave things alone."

"You didn't know your limits the other night when you held me back from Aydan," I said.

"Or did I? I'm still here," he said, checking out both sides of his hand to be sure.

"I suppose," I said.

"If we aren't talking, then you need to get off my bed," he teased.

"The man who swore the blood oath to me tonight was Zahir. He was once one of my father's knights, but when the kingdom split, he along with a few others, supported Lancelot. I know now that madness had taken over my father spurred on by my Uncle's poison. I cannot speak his name, because he was forsaken," I said.

"I'm not forbidden to say their names. I've read the stories," he said.

"The stories don't tell everything. My father tried to erase them from history," I said.

"He's dark-skinned. Palamedes," Levi surmised.

"Yes," I confirmed. "And now he is doomed to walk in the land of angels and demons. He came into Shady Grove that way. He promised to watch that way for me."

"That's handy," Levi said. "Which one made you sad?"

"What do you mean?"

"Thinking about the forsaken made you sad. One in particular," he said.

"I've always said that I've never lied to you, but that isn't true. This truth I've never told anyone," I said. "Jeremiah knew. I'm certain Tennyson knows. Tonight, Zahir reminded me."

"Grace," he said turning my face to his. "You have never lied to me. Even this doesn't feel like a lie. It's more like a story you couldn't tell for whatever reason." His thumb brushed over my cheek, then his hand sank to my neck.

A memory awoke in my head.

The touch of a man.

This touch.

Just like this.

"Levi, I..."

"Don't. You don't have to," he urged.

I jumped away from Levi's touch. Backing away from the couch, I stammered over my words. "I can't..."

"It's okay." He stood, reaching for me.

"No. Please, no," I said. He didn't listen. Pulling me into his arms, I shook with memories that I had never allowed myself to ponder. The memories of what truly drove me from the Otherworld. My banishment.

CHAPTER EIGHTEEN

Levi slept in the chair across from my bed. I watched him rest thinking about him guiding me to the bed last night. He asked no more questions. No words in my head. I had climbed into the bed and fallen asleep without him disturbing me at all. I wasn't surprised to see him still here. Glancing at the clock, I realized it was still early. I stretched my feet to the floor slowly. He didn't budge, sleeping hard. I grabbed the blanket off the end of the bed to cover him up as I padded by it.

Before I put it over him, I reached out to him to see if he was playing possum on me. He wasn't. I found the peaceful sound of his brain at rest. I tried to resist the urge to touch his face but failed. As my fingers brushed the scar on his cheek, he moaned opening his deep blues to me.

"Grace." His voice just above a whisper.

"Got you a blanket."

Reaching up to my hand on his cheek, he placed his palm over mine.

"Keep going," I urged with a grin on my face.

"You like this," she protested.

"You like this," I countered.

"I still don't know what possessed me," she huffed.

"My undeniable charm," I offered.

"Not hardly. More like lonely, sexually charged fairy," she said.

"If you had been so sexually charged, why didn't I get any?" I asked, even though I knew the answer. I didn't know the answer then, nor would I for a long time, but she was right. This moment was important in our history. A moment she gave to me for no reason whatsoever other than she just needed it. And, so did I. *"Grace."*

"Hmm?"

"Keep going," I urged. She smiled widely for me, and I was lost in her all over again.

Instead of throwing the blanket over his head, which I resisted the urge to do, I crawled up in his lap and buried my face in his neck. He grabbed the blanket, laying it over us, then wrapped his arms around me with a sigh. I felt his heart beating hard in his chest. He didn't know what to say, and neither did I.

It wasn't the most comfortable position for either of us. The chair was large enough, but it didn't matter. The comfort I needed I found wrapped up in his arms. Levi. My best friend. My bard.

We weren't there long before little feet padded up to the door. Winnie stood outside the door for a moment before she knocked.

"What's she waiting on?" Levi asked.

"Dunno," I answered.

Finally, after a few minutes, she knocked. "Momma."

Leaning up, I kissed Levi on the cheek. "Time to be a mom," I said.

"You are a great mom," he said, as I backed off of his lap to the floor. He sighed again.

"Come in, Winnie," I said.

She opened the door slowly with her eyes on the bed. She slowly turned to where I stood next to Levi in the chair. "Oh, hey, Uncle Levi. You were quiet, Momma. I thought you were asleep."

"No, I'm awake," I said. "Are you hungry?"

"Yes, but when I went downstairs, Aydan was talking to a man I didn't know. It scared me," she said. "I didn't want to burn him, so I came up here."

She had stood at the door trying to calm down before she came into the room with me. My little Phoenix was trying to control her powers.

"Good girl. That's Callum, and he's going to be staying with us," I said.

"Callum. He's a wolf," she said.

"Yes, he is. How did you know?" I asked.

"He smells like Mark," she replied. Interesting. She could smell the shifters. Levi raised an eyebrow catching it too.

"I'm going to change clothes, then I'll come downstairs," I said.

"I'll go down with you, Winnie," Levi said, standing up. He handed me the blanket. "Thank you, Grace." He leaned over, kissed my forehead, then left with Winnie.

"I must be losing my mind," I muttered.

"*Can't lose something you don't have, crazy woman,*" he said.

"*Bite me,*" I replied.

"*Next time,*" he answered.

Instead of being intimidated or uncomfortable, it made me laugh.

After a shower and a change of clothes, I joined Levi, Winnie, Callum, and Aydan in the living room. Levi pointed at my cell phone.

"You have missed calls," he said.

I picked it up looking at the number I didn't recognize. "I wonder who this was," I pondered.

"Probably Nick since he said he would call you," Levi offered.

"I didn't give him my number," I said.

"He must have it already," Levi replied. "*Bastard.*"

"You have my number," I said.

"So?"

"So, don't be jealous," I teased.

He didn't answer, but he looked up toward my bedroom at the other end of the house. I knew what he meant. After giving him that moment, he would never be jealous of Dominick again.

Suddenly, his eyes shot to the front door.

"Aydan, get your sister and go upstairs," Levi ordered. "Callum go with them."

Aydan looked at me for reassurance. "Go!"

Aydan grabbed Winnie and ran up the stairs with Callum on his heels, as someone started pounding on the front door.

"You stay back," Levi ordered. It wasn't the time to argue with him.

He slowly walked to the door. The guitar on his arm thrummed with a deep warning tone. I felt the protective power of an intense ward flow out of him slowly surrounding the house. He reached into the closet beside the front door, producing Excalibur.

The pounding at the door continued as I drew in my own power feeding off his. The ward itself drew power to it, feeding us.

The door blew into splinters as Atohi bounded inside with his fists raised.

"Where is he?" he spat at Levi.

"You have crossed the warded threshold of the Queen of the Exiles," Levi warned, lifting Excalibur.

"Your damn wards don't mean anything to me," he said. "I've still got power." He lifted his hand, palm forward to Levi.

"Don't do this, Atohi. Whatever is the problem, we will fix it," Levi shouted at him.

"I want the white wolf," he said. "His blood is owed to me."

"Over my dead body," I snarled at him.

Dominick appeared at the door behind Atohi. For a moment, I felt alarmed, but I saw his face. "May I enter?" he asked.

"Yes," Levi immediately answered. "Where is Troy?"

"He's coming. I'm faster," Dominick said. My eyes drifted from his face to the rest of him. Completely naked. He'd run here as a wolf, chasing Atohi.

"He can't stop me. I'm not a wolf. I'm First People. The white wolf's blood is mine to take," he said. "Give him to me."

"Atohi, if you think that she will hesitate to put you down, you are wrong. I know she can," Dominick warned him.

"Not if I stop him first," Levi said, as Excalibur sang in his hand.

"It is my right, by law," Atohi claimed.

"Leave this house," I said. "Last chance."

"You heard her. Leave," Aydan said at the top of the steps.

"Aydan," I said, turning to him in a panic.

"Thunderbird. This is of no concern to you," Atohi said with a calm voice.

"Aydan," I repeated his name, but his eyes were fixed on the midnight wolf.

"It is my concern. He asked me for help. Explained everything. He is my friend, and the blood debt was paid by his father," Aydan said.

"Blood debt! What the hell is going on?" I asked.

"I am due his entire line. They must all die by my hands. I deserve justice. The white wolf is the last. Give him to me," Atohi demanded again.

"No," Aydan replied. "Leave this house or suffer the consequences."

"You aren't old enough to make that call, Yas Shikoba," Atohi protested.

"I am, and I do," Aydan said defiantly. He may have looked like his father, but I was pretty sure he got that backbone from me.

Atohi didn't listen. He lunged past Levi toward the stairs, but before he hit the first step, my father's sword-actually my bard's sword- jutted out from his chest. The gleaming white light pierced through him.

"I may not be old like you, Atohi, but I know right from wrong. You never learned that lesson. Perhaps the Great Spirit will have mercy on you," Aydan said, as he descended the stairs. He stood before Atohi as he gasped for air. Levi did not withdraw the sword.

"My children will avenge me," he rasped as he sputtered blood.

"The cycle ends here," Aydan said. "I'll see to it."

Atohi's body slumped as he drew his last breath. Something in his face knew that Aydan would keep his promise. His death would not be avenged. Levi jerked the sword back, allowing his body to hit the floor.

I looked down at the body, then back up to Aydan. "Start talking, young man," I said.

He grinned, "You are so severe, Mom."

"Aydan, you knew that he was after Callum?" I asked.

"Yes, Callum told me last night after he learned that I was the Thunderbird. It is my duty to make sure that problems are resolved. That our people handle things properly. Fortunately for Atohi, his line will continue. Callum is the last of his family," Aydan said. "I promised to protect Callum by the laws of our people."

Callum peeked around the corner of the hallway. "Come out here, Callum," I said.

"Yes, ma'am," he replied.

"You aren't a normal shifter like the other wolves?" I asked.

"No, I'm more like Aydan and Atohi," he said looking down at the body. He closed his eyes and turned his head. Death meant something to him. It didn't seem to faze Aydan which was concerning.

"I've been trying to call you," Dominick interrupted.

"Yeah, thanks," I said, dismissing him.

"Grace, we tried to warn you," Troy said arriving at my door. "Damn you are fast." He said to Dominick with a grin, and he responded with an arrogant smile.

"There is a dead man in my house," I said flatly.

"Aydan, you and Callum keep Winnie upstairs. Play unicorns or something. Keep her busy while we get this cleaned up," Levi ordered.

"Sure. Come on, Cal," Aydan said.

"We will take care of it, Grace," Troy said. "You surprised us last night at the fights. I've not been trying to keep it from you. I thought the fights were well known and you just chose to stay away. I would never do anything behind your back."

"No, but I didn't give you those guns so I could stare down the barrel of one," I said. Levi grunted in agreement.

"It was the heat of the moment. I would have never shot you. If anything, I wanted to be able to make a move on Callum if he didn't obey my command for your protection," he said.

"It seems to me that even though he's not your kind, that he has submitted to your authority," I replied.

"He is a good boy. I should have seen what was going on with him and Atohi," he said.

"Do you think the elders will be upset?" I asked.

"I better call Remy and tell him what happened," Levi said.

"Amanda is on her way with one of the squad cars so we can move the body. Let us know if the elders want it," Troy said as the rumble of an engine approached outside. He turned to go out and meet Amanda.

Dominick walked over to be sure that Atohi was no longer breathing. He looked up at me with concern in his eyes. "I tried to get here as fast as I could," he said. "I'm sorry I didn't stop him before he came in your home."

"We handled it," I said.

"I'm still sorry," he said.

"I forgive you, Nick."

He grinned, "I didn't say you could call me Nick."

"Please," I scoffed. "Get this body out of my house."

I'd seen enough of the body myself. My stomach lurched with nausea, and I left Dominick in the living room with Levi. In the kitchen, I grabbed a glass filling it with water from the faucet. I took a couple of sips when I felt Levi walk up behind me.

"You okay?" he asked quietly.

"Yeah," I said, taking another sip of water.

"I think our security could use some work," he said.

"I agree. Perhaps we need some live guards outside of the magical wards," I said, turning to face him. I hadn't realized how close he was, but it was clear when his hand found my cheek.

"I will never let anything get to you or the children," he said. "Ever."

"I believe you, but just remember that sometimes we can't prepare for everything. I'm not the most powerful thing out there," I said. "Neither are you."

"Thank you for this morning," he said. "I had resolved to sit back and wait on you. It was getting harder and harder for me. I've not been in control the last few days, and I'm sorry. I'm still waiting. I'll wait forever."

I turned my mouth to his palm and kissed it gently. "It won't be long," I said. He exhaled the tension that had built up with Atohi and with me.

"Hey, Levi, give us a hand," Dominick called from the other room.

"That damn wolf needs to back off. He knows I'm in here with you," Levi said.

"You are cute when you are jealous," I said.

"So, I need to be more jealous?" he asked.

"No," I replied firmly. "Go help them." He was attractive enough without adding to it.

CHAPTER NINETEEN

WORD SPREAD QUICKLY ABOUT ATOHI. IT WASN'T LONG before my home was filled with concerned knights and friends. I sat back in my recliner as Levi perched himself on the arm of the chair.

"I spoke to the elders. They would like his body. They would like to speak to Aydan about his decision to break the blood feud between the families. The thunderbirds used to police these types of things to prevent the mass murders of families. This one has been going on for quite a while. With Dylan here, I'm not sure he had any way of knowing about it. Aydan did the right thing," Remy said, as he sat on the couch with Tabitha.

Aydan and Callum leaned on the wall between the dining room and living room. I saw the pride in Aydan's eyes when Remy said he'd done the right thing. Looking at the boys, I realized that my son had found a friend. Probably one that would last a lifetime. A common bond between two beings was something that surpassed even death.

"Do you want us to suspend the fights?" Troy asked.

"I hope not. There is little to no entertainment in this town," Tennyson said.

"As long as you keep it under control, I don't see why you have to stop. I understand the need and how you are using it to build the pack," I said.

"It is a great tool for the future when we need to make a move on Brockton. I know exactly who my best fighters are. I know who to send out if we get attacked, and who to leave behind for the protection of the rest. Each one has special skills," he said.

"What about Callum?" I asked. "Is he part of the pack?"

Troy hung his head.

"I'd rather stay here," Callum spoke up.

"He cannot come back, Grace. No matter what Atohi did to him, he broke the rules. I can't make an exception," Troy said.

He could make an exception if he really wanted. If he was truly in control, his word should be the end of anything, but perhaps I didn't understand the full workings of the pack. Perhaps I didn't know what damage going against his word would do to his authority.

"He is welcome to stay here with us. Levi and I discussed more security. The living, breathing kind," I said.

"I think that is an excellent idea," Astor spoke up.

"I agree," Finley said.

"One of us should be here at all times," Tennyson added.

"I want to go outside. This is boring," Winnie said from her spot on the floor. I supposed it was a tad boring for a seven-year-old. Mark who had come with Amanda sat on the floor next to her even though she wasn't paying him any attention.

"I've got her," Aydan said, crossing the room to his sister. "Come on, Wildfire. Let's go outside."

Bramble and Briar buzzed behind as Aydan, Callum, Mark, and Winnie headed for the back door. Rufus remained at my feet.

I was sure he didn't like the other dogs in the house, but he wasn't going outside with Aydan either.

"Your son is impressive," Remy said. "He will be a formidable leader for our people. We have sorely missed having one. It wasn't Dylan's fault. He was saddled with two responsibilities with no one to guide him."

"His parents didn't teach him?" I asked, showing how little I knew about Dylan's birth and parents.

"No, they died shortly after his birth," Remy said. "Our people shunned them for their union, then shunned him for the dual roles. Dylan found his own way. It took him a while, but once he arrived here, it seemed like he'd finally found his purpose in life."

A tear rolled down my cheek, and Levi reached down to wipe it away for me.

"Any word from Winter?" Levi asked.

"No. But Summer will make a move soon. I suggest we send Astor into Summer to the hacienda near the tree. Perhaps he can get more info than I can at the moment. My contact is heavily involved with Rhiannon's preparations, and I haven't been able to contact him," Tennyson said.

"What if we jump into Winter, and Rhiannon changes her course to here?" I asked.

"Then I will be here to defend the Vale," Tennyson said.

"As will I," Jenny added. "There are those who will remain that can fight."

"The pack will be here under Dominick's control," Troy said.

"About that," Dominick interjected.

"What?" Troy asked.

"Perhaps I should go with Grace and Levi, and you stay here," Dominick suggested.

"No," Troy said with no further discussion.

But I wondered why. "Why?" I asked. Dominick looked to Troy for permission to speak, but Troy shook his head.

"It's a pack matter," Troy said.

"You know there was a time when you didn't care about a pack," I said, reminding Troy of his lone wolf status.

"Things have changed. You helped me see that. Don't make me regret it, Grace," he said with the slightest tease in his voice.

"You don't regret the pack. You just regret dealing with me," I teased back.

"We all do," Levi said, causing the room to erupt in laughter. I pushed him hard trying to topple him off the arm of the chair, but the muscles in his legs strained to keep his balance on the arm. I gave up after a moment.

"Alright. All of you get out of my house," I said. "I've seen enough of your ugly mugs for today."

"Be ready for the call, Grace. It won't be long," Tennyson warned.

"We will be ready," Levi answered.

We spoke to everyone as they left. Luther and Betty had called to check on us, but decided to stay in town since they were working the diner. Nestor had waited patiently outside while we had our meeting. I told him to come in, but he refused.

After everyone left, I found him standing outside watching Winnie and Mark play with the brownies. Amanda called for Mark to leave. He tried to speak to Winnie, but she crossed her arms and looked away from him.

"Bye, Miss Grace," he said, running past me.

"Bye, Mark," I said.

"She's becoming more like you every day," Nestor said.

"Most mothers would be proud, but I suppose I'm getting what I'm due for all the rebellious years. For going against my father's instructions and desires," I said.

"He was happy you were here and not there," Nestor said.

"Later on, yes he was. But I'll never forget the disappointment on his face the day he caught me coming back to the Otherworld after a trip into the human realm," I said.

"It wasn't that you were gone. It was who you were with," he said.

I paused for a moment wondering what Nestor knew about my banishment. Did he know the truth or the story I had always told everyone?

"It was because I disobeyed him. He felt betrayed," I said.

"Because you were teasing human men?" Nestor asked.

Nestor only knew the story I'd always told. It was a relief to me. I had almost told Levi about it. If anyone deserved to know the truth, it was Levi. Nestor and the rest could come later. Watching Levi across the yard speaking to Dominick, I wondered if I could ever tell him the truth. He was right. The pain of it was equal to the loss of Dylan. If I were to ever give my heart to Levi, he needed to know the true state of it. He needed to know the scars and bruises.

I decided to dismiss those dark thoughts, and have a word with my daughter about her attitude. I joined her on the swings.

"Swing high, Momma," she said.

"I will in a minute, but we need to talk," I said.

"What about?" she asked.

"I know you are upset with Mark. I know you are trying to learn what it's like to be a Phoenix. I'm going to help you as much as I can, but you have to remember that you are a princess. You are my daughter, and we need to learn to treat everyone with respect. If you are mad at Mark, then fine, but don't be hateful," I said.

"He keeps apologizing about the thing at the wedding," she said.

"And you should forgive him," I said. "Do you think he means it?"

"He does, but I don't want to forgive him," she said.

"You realize that burning Corbin would have been a bad thing to do, right?" I asked.

"Yes."

"Then he did the right thing," I offered.

"And?"

"You were wrong, Winnie. You need to learn to admit when you are wrong," I said. "It took your momma a long time to learn that. I spent a very, very long time being lonely because I couldn't admit when I was wrong. I couldn't forgive those who stood against me. I don't want you to grow up like that."

She swayed back and forth on the swing. Perhaps I'd gotten too deep for her.

"You were lonely?" she asked.

"Yes, very lonely until I met your daddy," I said. "He made me remember what it was like to love and forgive. We all make mistakes, but we only become better when we are willing to admit it."

She stopped swinging. Her eyes tracked Levi as he walked toward us.

"Do you love Uncle Levi? Like you loved Daddy?" she asked.

Lord have mercy. This wasn't the conversation I wanted to have with her.

"I love your Uncle Levi, but it's very different from the way I loved Dylan," I said.

"So, you aren't going to marry him?" she asked.

"*Stay over there with Nestor please,*" I warned Levi. He stopped right next to Nestor. "*It's okay. Just a Mom and daughter talk.*"

"*Okay,*" he nodded with understanding.

"Winnie, I don't know what the future will be for us. I just know that Levi and Dylan are two very different men. You cannot love someone the same way you loved someone else. Let me ask you this. Did you love your mother, Bethany?" I asked.

"Yes," she said quietly. She reached up to grab the keys hanging around her neck.

"Do you love me the same way you loved her?" I asked.

"Yes. I mean, I dunno," she said as she looked down at the keys in her hand. "You are different than she was. You care about if I'm being bad."

"Levi and your Daddy are different like that. I love them differently," I said.

"You care if Levi is being bad?" she asked.

"Absolutely," I laughed.

"What's so funny?" she asked.

"Nothing," I giggled.

"I suppose you could marry Uncle Levi and it would be okay with me," she said.

"Oh, really?" I said.

"Yeah, because he cares if you are being bad, too," she said.

I died laughing because, bless her little pea pickin' heart, she had no idea how much truth she had just spoken. Dylan kept me reeled in, but Levi tried to keep me from getting out of hand way before I tossed more line out there.

"Now can we swing high?" she asked.

"Yes!" I replied.

"Come push me, Uncle Levi," she shouted.

Levi ran over and pushed us both. I watched Callum and Aydan sitting on the back-porch drinking sodas. They laughed and joked like boys do. Nestor joined us at the swings chatting about the weather and the little things. It was nice to talk about nothing, instead of planning for war or marriages. It wouldn't be long before that call would come, and we would step into the Other-world. Some of us might not come back.

CHAPTER TWENTY

When I stepped into the diner with Aydan and Callum, there was only one other customer. Dominick smiled as the boys took seats down from him. I sat down right next to him.

"Hi," I said.

"Um, hello, Grace," he said. I'd already made him uncomfortable.

"You warned me multiple times about Atohi," I said.

"Yes." He slumped his shoulders and looked down at his coffee cup.

"Then why is it, that it got as far as it did? You knew he was bad," I said.

"It was an instinct, and I had no proof," he said. "The fight was the first time he slipped."

"Did you share this instinct with Troy?" I asked.

"I did," he said.

"And?"

"And I'd prefer not to discuss it with you," he said boldly. I knew he didn't want to cross his alpha which was honorable, but if there were problems in the ranks, I wanted to know.

"Okay. Let's just say if you get that instinct again, you come to me. You tell me if no one else will listen. I trust your instincts just as much as I trust his. I won't cross either of you. I won't pit you against him, but if there is something that you think I should know, I will pay more attention next time," I said.

He didn't speak as he twirled the half cup of coffee around in his hands.

"You want more, honey?" Betty asked holding a fresh pot.

"No, thank you, Betty," he said.

"Grace, you ordering?" she asked.

"No, just feed those boys," I said.

"Gotcha," she said, leaving us alone.

"You okay?" I asked.

He looked at me eye to eye finally. "Why do you trust me now?"

"You've proven yourself," I said.

"I'm still proving myself," he said.

"Not to me."

"Thank you."

"No, thank you. And I'll try to answer my phone next time," I grinned.

"Next time it might be a social call," he said.

"That answer is still no," I teased.

"Can't blame me for trying," he said.

"No, I can't. Just stay off Levi's radar," I warned.

"We've talked."

"Oh, really?"

"Yeah, we reached an agreement," he said.

"And what, pray tell, was that agreement?" I asked.

"He said I was welcome to try, but that you would always tell me no," he said. "He was right."

"He learned that trick from Dylan," I said.

"Oh?"

"Yep. There was a time when Levi was on the no end of the equation," I admitted.

"Isn't he still on the no end?" Dominick asked.

I didn't answer. "Have a good day, Nick."

"You too, Grace."

I hadn't walked out to the stone circle in a while. I hadn't had the need. My connection to the Otherworld as heir to the throne provided me with all the power that I needed. With my father gone, there wasn't much reason to walk out there.

Winnie was still at school, then would go visit Luther after school for her Phoenix lessons. I dropped the boys off at the work-site with Levi because Remy needed more hands to finish the housing units they were working on. I took the opportunity to visit the circle.

Walking through the woods, I felt the chill of the approaching winter. Somewhere in the distance a storm brewed. I touched the trees as I walked along. Each one welcomed me. Some commented on my absence. When I reached the circle, I was surprised to see it wasn't overgrown. The grass was neatly trimmed and the stones stood as proudly as they had before.

A hum of power resounded in the outer stones as I passed them. That's when I heard the brownies. It started with the slap of bare hand on skin.

"Oh, yes, Daddy," a female voice said that didn't sound like Briar. Bramble was going to be in deep shit. I heard his little grunts before I reached the center stone. On the back side of the stone, Briar sat with a tiny whip while Bramble pounded a purple haired pixie. I assumed this was the infamous Thistle.

"Harder, Bramble," Briar said, smacking him with the whip. He yelped, then pounded harder.

When I started giggling, they finally realized I was there. The purple haired fairy jumped behind Bramble who held his hands over his little prick.

"You are interrupting," Briar informed me.

"My bad. I didn't know my circle had become the local BDSM club," I laughed.

"It isn't funny," Bramble huffed. Thistle giggled. Apparently, she and I had something in common.

"I'm truly sorry. I was just out here for a walk. Surely there is somewhere better to do this," I suggested.

"Why? You never come out here anymore. At least until today. And Levi keeps the grass cut," Briar replied.

"I see your point. Levi cuts the grass?" I asked.

"Yes. He opens the portal, hauls the mower through, then mows it at least once a week," Bramble reported. "It didn't seem like something you needed to know."

I had assigned Bramble and Briar to keep an eye on things, but with Winnie gone most of the time, I see that they had managed to find other activities to keep them busy.

"I guess we are finished for today," Briar said.

"I didn't finish!" Bramble protested.

"Look. You guys go back to doing whatever that was, and I'll just walk back to the house. But do me a favor and stay off the center stone," I said.

"Oh, Lilith won't let us do it on the stone," Bramble said. Briar smacked his bare butt with the whip.

"Shush," she hissed.

"Hold up," I said. "Lilith was here?"

"Yes, she made us get off the stone. Said she could hear us in the tree," Bramble said. "She also told us not to tell you."

"So, Lilith can hear what is going on through the stone," I surmised.

"You are toast, and it's not my fault," Briar said.

The stone began to glow with the familiar blue light. I stepped away from it before the goddess herself showed up.

"Bloody hell," Bramble murmured. Thistle took flight and skittered off into the woods.

Lilith appeared above the stone, staring down at the little brownies.

"If you weren't her property, I would fry you where you stand," she scowled.

They both bowed deeply to her. "Forgive me, O, great goddess of the tree. I'm just a poor, blue balled brownie," Bramble murmured.

She quirked a smile at me, then dismissed the little ones. "Be gone!"

Bramble and Briar shot out toward the same direction as Thistle which was not toward my house. Hopefully, poor Mr. Blue Balls would get his relief.

"Before you ask, yes, it's true. I can hear through the stone," she said.

"How much do you hear?" I asked.

"That depends on how hard I am listening," she replied.

"You are a goddess. Don't you hear everything anyway?" I asked.

"I am not omniscient," she replied. "I wonder. Why did you walk this way, Grace?"

"I dunno. Seemed like something to do," I said. I hadn't given it much thought. I spent most of my walk here thinking of the good times that Dylan and I had surrounding the stones like when he finally opened up and told me much about his abilities and why he had hidden them from me. Even then I didn't know the whole truth.

"You are answering me without answering me," she said.

I rolled my eyes at the goddess. She had proven to be wishy-washy. I wasn't interested in appeasing her ego.

"You almost told Levi about the forsaken," she said.

"I did," I confirmed. "And?"

"Why did you stop?" she asked.

"I didn't want to talk about it. It's not like I can," I said. "The curse is still intact. I can feel it."

"If you took the Winter throne, you could erase it," she said.

She had told me something that I had just assumed to be true. As the monarch, I would have complete control over the banished and forsaken. I had a whole lot of pardoning to do, starting with Lancelot.

"Do you think of him?" she asked.

"No," I replied.

"You are a liar," she said. "You think of him often. Every time Levi gets close, you think of him."

"I think of Dylan," I contradicted her.

She laughed scornfully. "You lie to yourself. Do you not wonder now if he is in the tree?"

"I assume that he is," I replied. "If you don't mind, I need to get back to the house."

"He is coming," she smiled.

"Who is coming?" I asked.

"He is," she laughed as she suddenly got a case of crazy eye.

I turned away from her to leave the circle, when a large white deer with huge antlers stepped out into the clearing. My breath caught in my chest. But then I heard his voice.

"Grace, who are you talking to?" Levi asked.

"Lilith," I replied, looking behind me to see that the stone had faded. She was gone. I looked back to the deer. *"What the hell?"*

The creature took several steps into the circle, then lowered his head to me. I reached up to brush its cheek, then noticed the scar from above the eye to below its jaw.

"I'm a stag," he said.

"I see," I said out loud. "When did you learn to do this?"

"Dunno. Just thought I'd give it a try," he said from his deer mouth.

"Okay. That's freaky as hell," I said.

Then he laughed, which was even more weird. I stared in amazement.

"You look stunned," he said. "Now you can put on that horn and run with me."

"Um, no," I said. "Unicorn is very different than a white stag. At least folks around these parts have seen albino deer."

"One day you will," he said as he morphed back into my bard. "Hi."

"Hi."

"What are you doing out here?"

"Just went for a walk. Found the brownie threesome. That left a mark in my memory that I didn't need," I said.

"Oh, yeah. Briar and her whip," he said.

"What? How did you know?" I asked. "She said you cut the grass."

"That's how I know. I've caught them too. It's freaking hilarious. Briar the Dominatrix," he laughed. It echoed around the stones. A rich, full laugh. He quickly sobered realizing that I was watching him closely. "Are you okay?"

"Yes. She just brought up some bad memories," I said.

"That seems to be happening a lot," he said.

"It does. I don't know why now all of the sudden it matters," I wondered.

"Why what matters?" he asked.

"The forsaken," I said.

"Oh, like Palamedes," he said. I cringed when he spoke the name. A name I couldn't say. There were eight others. Friends and supporters of Lancelot. Enemies to my father. "Who are the others?"

"Ask Tennyson. He can still speak their names, but I doubt he will. They are all dead," I said.

"Do you remember them?" he asked.

"Just one. The rest were executed before I was born," I said.

"The one. Who was he?" he asked.

"Please don't ask me anymore. The force that binds my tongue weighs upon me each time you ask. One day, when I take back the throne, I will tell their stories. You can write them down," I said. "They deserve to be remembered for their loyalty and love." A lump grew in my throat as I spoke. I didn't know any of them. Except one.

He took my hand, and we walked back toward the house.

"Go ahead and ask," I said sensing he had more to say, but forced himself to keep quiet.

"If Zahir was executed before you were born, why did he seem familiar to you?" he asked.

"I don't know. He just did," I said. I knew his and a few of the other's stories. The rest I could never dig up in this world. After realizing that Tennyson was still alive, I just assumed he knew all of their stories. After the encounter with Zahir, I knew that he did.

"I talked to Dominick," he said, changing the subject as the house came into view.

"When?" I asked.

"After he saw you in the diner," Levi said. Cutting my eyes to him, I saw the grin teasing the edges of his mouth. "He gave me the impression that you told him that you and I were an item."

"That is not what I said," I protested. He died laughing, knowing that I hadn't said such a thing.

"Perhaps you should clarify," he suggested.

I tried pulling my hand away from him, but he wouldn't let me go. "Levi," I warned.

"What?" he continued to grin.

"I just implied that things were different between us," I said.

He reeled me back to him, inch by inch grasping my arms even though I fought him. I wasn't fighting very hard.

"What is different, Gloriana?" he asked. I shuddered at the use of my real name.

"Nothing," I said by the time, he had me inches away from his body.

Wrapping his arm around my waist, he dragged me the rest of the way. He looked down at me with those playful blue eyes. "Nothing at all?"

"Nothing," I whispered.

He dipped his head so that his cheek brushed mine. "Nothing?" he whispered in my ear.

Goosebumps rose up on my skin. "Levi." I tried to protest, but it came out more like desire than disgust.

"Hmm?" he moaned as he hovered his lips over mine. I was mesmerized by his tone, the strength of his hands, and the movements of his body.

His cell phone started to ring in his pocket. Then mine.

"Fuck," he muttered, but didn't move to answer it.

A glittering portal opened in front of the house, and Tennyson stepped through it.

"It's time," he called out to us.

I closed my eyes to shake off the effects of the Love Talker.

"Shit," I said.

"Double shit," he added. I opened my eyes to see him grinning. "We will get back to this after."

"Um, okay," I said.

"Now, Levi!" Tennyson ordered.

Levi shot him the bird.

"You copying my moves now?" I asked.

"I want your everything," he replied. Love talker to the end.

CHAPTER TWENTY-ONE

"Winnie is with Luther, and the boys were at the work site," I said as we rushed to the house.

"I brought Callum and Aydan home when I came back," he said.

Tennyson waited for us impatiently. "Jenny is on the way," he said.

"Winnie is with Luther," I said to Tennyson.

"I will take care of everything. The two of you need to get to the maze," he said. "Here, Levi, take this." He pulled a large ring off his finger. Celtic knots circled the band on each side of a large emerald stone.

"No, I can dispel magic," Levi protested, but slipped Tennyson's ring on his finger.

"Not hers," Tennyson said. "Get to the maze. The others will meet you there."

Aydan and Callum ran out of the house. "Mom?"

"Aydan!" I said running up to him. I wrapped my arms around him. "It's time for us to go. Promise me that you will take care of your sister."

"Yeah, I will, but you have to come back," he said.

"I'll bring her back," Levi said. "Helmet or not. We are coming back."

Stepping back from him, I looked him in the eyes. Dylan's cobalt blue eyes. "I love you, Aydan. Take care of Callum, too."

"Whatever. I've got to look out for him," Callum said. I reached over and patted Callum on the cheek.

"Thank you," I said.

"Aw, Mom," Aydan protested.

"Grace," Tennyson urged.

"I need to see Winnie," I said.

"We won't be gone long," Levi insisted. "You take care of her." Levi added to my request.

"I will," Aydan assured him.

"You take care of all of them," Levi said to Tennyson.

"I've got back-up coming," he said looking down the lane. Two fauns walked up the drive side-by-side. I hadn't seen Devin in a while, but he and his father, Joey Blankenship walked up to us.

"Time to go?" Joey asked.

"Yes," I said. "Thank you for coming."

"I've heard that you might have a job opening in the security department," he said. "Consider this a trial run."

"We will talk about it when I get back," I said.

"Now! You need to go now," Tennyson said, becoming more frustrated.

Levi ran up to the house, then trotted back with Excalibur. "I need my armor," he said.

"It's at the maze," Tennyson said. "Go!"

Levi grabbed my hand, and we skipped to the hedge maze in the forest where I had first saw my brother smuggling goods from Winter. He stood next to Troy, waiting for us.

"Where is Astor?" Troy asked.

"He's a newlywed. Give him a minute," Levi said.

"We don't have a minute. We need to go," Finley said.

"You sound like Tennyson," I said.

"I don't want to be there any longer than we have to be. The sooner we leave. The sooner we can come back," Finley said.

Luther swooped down from above with his fiery wings spreading out behind him. "Jenny picked up Winnie, and she is taking her to your house," he reported.

"Okay," I said sadly. I had hoped to see my daughter before we left.

"*Don't worry. We are coming back,*" Levi insisted. "Put your game face on."

"It's on," I protested.

"Well, then, put your armor on," he said, as Finley handed him his armor. My brother, Luther, and Troy were already decked out. Troy wore a Kevlar vest with black t-shirt and cargo pants. Black combat boots reached up his shins and were tied tightly.

Luther didn't need armor. His dried lava skin looked as hard as obsidian.

Finley wore his blue winter armor with the stag head and triquetra symbol. I thought about Levi shifting to a stag when I saw it. How did Finley know? Or perhaps he didn't. Perhaps it was just a strange coincidence.

Finally, Astor stepped through a glittering portal with his armor already on. "I'm ready," he announced.

"You sure?" I asked. His cheeks looked flushed.

"Nothing I can't finish when I get back," he said with a smile.

"How long have they been married?" Finley asked.

"Long enough to pop that cherry a few times over," I said. The group chuckled while Astor blushed and grumbled.

"Not the time or place, Grace," he said.

"It's the perfect time and place. We are about to jump into unknown danger to steal a helmet which already belongs to me in a land filled with wild fairies. It just happens to be ruled by my insane uncle and some crazy ORCs. Perfect time," I said.

"I agree, Sunkist," Levi added.

"You would, Band Geek," Astor huffed.

"He had a comeback!" Levi exclaimed, patting Astor on the back. I laughed. Astor seemed quite satisfied with himself. Then, Finley spoiled them moment.

"Aw, come on, that's enough. Let's get going," Finley said.

"What's the plan?" Luther asked.

"We go in. Give Grace enough time to track the helmet, grab it, and get out without getting caught," Levi said.

"Or dead," Finley added.

"The helmet is not worth any of your lives," I said.

"If we find it, we must get it out. It cannot fall into Mordred's hands," Astor said.

"Or Rhiannon's," I said.

"Armor. Now," Levi ordered.

"Bossy little cuss," I said.

My winter armor appeared in a rush of cold wind. I decided the crown wasn't needed in this application. My arrival was not as a queen, but as a thief. One day I'd bounce into that joint, crown and all, just like it was a bar on Saturday night. But not today.

We picked the hedge maze as a jumping off point because we knew where it opened. Any other point would be difficult to manage since Levi had only been in a few places in Winter.

Reaching out with my senses as Levi positioned himself to open the portal, the wind whispered through my long platinum hair. The earth pulsed with life beneath my feet. Tiny snowflakes fell around us coating the ground with a light dust. The desire in my soul flamed to a steady burn. The desire to bring my Uncle down. To avenge the deaths, he'd caused. To free the fairies of Shady Grove. To do things right when no one else could.

Wind, earth, water, and fire. I was taking the power of the stones with me.

Levi twirled Excalibur in a large circle. The glittering portal appeared as his sweep completed the arch. A waft of the dank earthy smell of the Otherworld assaulted our noses. Inside the portal, I saw the empty room that once belonged to my father.

Troy stepped through with Driggs drawn. Finley lifted his sword just before he crossed over. I followed with Luther on my heels. Astor and Levi were the last to step through, but just as the circle closed. Dominick bounded through the opening.

"What the fuck are you doing?" Troy growled at him.

"You need me here," he said.

"I told you to stay behind," Troy said.

"Amanda is with the pack. They are protecting Grace's house and children," Dominick said. "I told you that I have to be here."

"Enough! It's too late now. Stop arguing," I warned. Pointing at Dominick, I said, "You are in deep shit. Deep doggy doo-doo."

"I know," he conceded.

"The way I see it, you are all in deep shit," a deep voice echoed through the empty room. The wall shimmered, and my Uncle stepped into sight. He'd been disguised by a glamour keeping him invisible to us.

Levi raised Excalibur which glowed in the darkness. Astor's sword illuminated us from behind.

"Gloriana, welcome home. Levi, it is a pleasure to see you again," he smirked, as two hulking ogres stepped up beside him. They stood over 8 feet tall with green skin marked with boils and oozing puss. One smacked his tree trunk-sized fist in his hand, while the other grinned so widely that drool dropped from his chin to the floor like a giant water balloon. "Kill them."

The ogres charged us, so we spread out in different directions to give them multiple targets. Luther took the first hit, but he bounced off a wall with wings unfurled in a fiery blossom.

My Uncle quietly slipped out of the door of the chamber, magically shutting the doors behind him. I could get through the ward, but we had to survive the eye-broccoli brothers. Running to the door, I watched over my shoulder as my knights readied themselves to fight the brutes. The power of Winter flooded over me like an avalanche. I was home, and home was happy to see me. Keeping one eye on the fight behind me, I started working to disable the wards on the door. It was a task more suited to Levi, but he had a sword to use.

One of the ogres wielded a large club at anyone close to him. A gigantor size compared to the clubs the Yule Lads used at the swamp battle. And wielded was a loose term to say that he swung it around hitting everything in the room except us.

"Levi, I'm going to need a suppressor!" Troy yelled out as the club-less ogre headed toward him. Troy stood tall holding Driggs out before him.

"Silence!" Levi yelled, unleashing a thrum across his tattoo.

Troy began firing one of the magical guns. Fiery bullets streaked across the room hitting the ogre in the chest. The cave beast screamed in silence as he pounded his chest to put out the fire. Levi's spell had silenced the entire room, not just the guns. Troy fired at the big guy again. The bullet dug deep into his skull. Flames shot out of his eyes, ears, and mouth. His final inaudible bellow died in a cloud of ash.

I stood in awe of the power of the guns. If only Dylan would have had the chance to...

"Grace!" Levi yelled, breaking the quiet.

Looking toward him, I realized the other monstrosity was headed toward me. I had been trained to fight. In fact, in my lifetime, I'd been in quite a few scuffles. It was time to show this crew what I could do. I met my brother's eyes, and finally, he smirked. Whatever foul mood he had been in evaporated when he realized, I was about to show off.

"Freeze!" Levi yelled along with a tinkling sound from the strings on his arm.

The spell only slowed the ogre for a moment as the ice chunks that formed around his feet shattered with the weight of his stomp.

"Come to Momma," I taunted. Reaching inside the breastplate of my armor, I withdrew two hilts. I gripped one in each hand and snarled at the beast. Forcing my winter power into the hilts, an icy blade grew by my command. No longer than a machete, the blade curved at the end leading to a point like a Bowie knife. I had practiced with all sorts of swords, but could never get the hang of a longer weapon. Short swords were just a little too bulky. The beauty of my icy blades was that I could change their shape at will.

At the last moment, the big, green oaf lunged toward me. I stepped sideways dragging the dagger in my left hand beside his neck. Black ichor rushed out of the gaping wound. He tumbled to the floor from the lunge that missed me. I jumped on his back and plunged both blades into his skull with a thunderous grunt. I snapped the ice blades off in his skull and waited for him to stop shuddering before I looked up.

Levi's mouth hung wide open. The others were wide-eyed.

"What the hell was that?" Dominick said.

"I don't know but that was sexy as fuck," Levi said, as his gap formed into a grin. "Where did you get those hilts?"

"I hide them in my bra," I grinned.

"That's my trailer park queen!" he laughed.

I winked at him, then turned to Troy. "Nice guns," I said.

"I want to shoot the other one now!" he smiled.

"Let's find a target for you," I said. "I feel the helmet. It's in my room. Well, my old room."

When I turned to go toward the warded door, I looked over to Levi knowing he could open them quicker than I could. He walked up next to me holding my father's sword. I grew two new blades on my hilts as he yelled, "Open sesame!"

"Really?" I muttered.

The force of the wind that opened the doors knocked them off their hinges.

"Shall we?" he said.

"Let's go," I replied.

Levi and I led the way while our knights followed close behind.

CHAPTER TWENTY-TWO

As we ran down the corridor, we met two more ogres which were quickly dispatched by Troy and Driggs. The second gun fired bullets of pure electricity which shocked the ogres like they were having a date with Old Yeller. The humans in Alabama used to do executions by electric chair. The damned thing was painted yellow. Old Yeller, they called it. These wild fairies met with a dose of southern justice fairy style. Dylan would have been proud.

However, the charred bodies stank so badly that I became nauseous.

"Damn, that stinks," Levi complained. "Stick with the fire one."

"I agree," I said, as we turned the last corner leading to my old chambers.

Thirty harpies stood between us and the door.

"Fuck a duck!" I yelled.

"I'm not fond of ducks," Levi said.

"Stand down," I ordered, hoping my claim to the throne was enough to control them.

"Queen Gloriana, you do not hold the throne in Winter. Until you do, you shall not pass. We will let you go, but you must turn back now," the harpy in the front said.

"Astraea, let us past. The fate of all the Otherworld depends upon it," Finley urged, stepping to the front of our group.

"Well, if it isn't Prince Penis," she mocked. The women behind her snickered at the name. I would have laughed in a different situation, but I decided to keep the nickname in my pocket for future use.

"This is serious, Astraea. Brockton will destroy the throne if he breaks down the veil," Finley said ignoring the taunt. The fact that Finley knew her name didn't surprise me. I was pretty sure he *knew* all the women in the Otherworld, and some of the men.

"We stand at the command of our King," she said.

"He's no King," I growled.

"You're no Queen," she countered.

"I am Queen of the Exiles, daughter of Oberon, heir to the throne of Winter," I said.

"Exiles! I hear you lived in a mobile home like a common wench. I hear that you adopted a human daughter. I hear you have a half-breed son by a dead bird," she said.

Leaning forward on my toes, I lifted my weapons with the icy blades pointed downward. "So be it," I said.

She countered by lifting her staff with the curved blade at the end. The women behind her mimicked her movements. She nodded at me like she was giving me permission to strike first. I got the drop on the ogre, but I knew better than to try to fight a flock of harpies.

Dropping the blades to the floor, she watched them hit and shatter. She missed the part where I pulled power from Winter, the water stone, and the wind stone forcing an icy blast in front of me which froze them all instantly.

I brushed frost off my hands then, picked up the hilts of my daggers. "What are we waiting on?" I asked.

"Are you going to let the rest of us do anything?" Finley asked.

"You guys got a couple of ogres," I said. "You can take the next one."

"I call dibs," Luther said.

"He beat you," I laughed at Finley.

"I'll get one. You will see," Finley assured me.

"Let's go. Don't touch them. I don't want them killed," I said.

Levi moved to the front, leading the way through the ice statues. We gingerly walked through the half-woman, half-bird creatures. It amazed me that they fought bare-breasted. Getting one of those sliced-off would hurt like the dickens.

"Are you staring at their boobs?" Levi asked.

I blushed, "Maybe." He laughed and shook his head. Holding our palms up to the door, we reached inside with magic to get a sense of what was on the other side. Looking at our hands side by side, my eyes focused on the diamond on my hand. It glittered in the earthy darkness of the Winter Otherworld. Levi's hand flexed as he felt inside the room beyond the door. It was a reminder of how his use of magic had grown. When he came to me, he didn't know much about it. I was supposed to teach him, but now the power he controlled outshone mine. "Just one?"

"I only feel one being in there. Feels familiar," Levi said.

"Alright. Open the doors," I said.

He raised his hands preparing for a spell. Pausing, I knew he was trying to think of another asinine spell command to use, but then he surprised me by lowering his hand to the door knob. He turned it quickly, and the door opened.

"It wasn't locked," he said.

"I see that," I smirked. He lifted Excalibur and stepped into my old bedroom. We had been here before when he pulled nails out of my leg. He also played a very long healing tune while my father's doctors tended my wounds. Dylan had been here too.

However, now the room was empty.

"Bath?" I asked.

"Yes," he said. Slowly we moved toward my favorite room in my father's castle. Hell, it was my favorite room in the Otherworld. My bathroom.

Standing in the center of the Roman style bath was a face I hadn't seen in a while. Steam rose from the water making the room hazy, but through it I could see her long black hair and piercing eyes. Her cheeks were covered with tracks of tears. The wet dress she wore exposed her body to us, leaving nothing to the imagination. She didn't have a bruise or mark on her. Upon her head, she wore my father's helmet, Goswhit.

Stephanie Davis had been saved from my wrath only to find herself imprisoned by the man she thought would become her king. Instead, he married her niece, Robin.

"Grace, please help me," she whimpered. "You know this is a trap."

I stared at her with indignation. I didn't care what kind of trauma she had been through, she had tried for months to tear Dylan and I apart. She brought Brockton into Shady Grove knowing who and what he was. Most of all, as a mother, I despised her. She used her son as a pawn in her games. Anger welled up inside of me as I lifted my fingers to snap her out of existence.

"No, wait!" Levi said, grabbing my hand.

My anger unleased on him. "Levi Rearden, this is not the time for you to turn into my conscious," I growled.

"He wants you to kill her. Just wait. He knows you would do it. Please listen to me," he said, trying to break through the anger and pain. Just seeing her brought back all the memories of Dylan and me.

"He's right, Grace. He put the helmet on me to lure you here.

He wants you to kill me, because he can't do it himself. He swore an oath to me. Breaking it would mean his death," she pleaded.

"Shut the fuck up right now!" I said, pointing at her.

"I know Dylan is dead. I'm so sorry. I'm so, so sorry. He was a wonderful man, and I kept you from him. I have been horrible, but please don't let Brockton win. Please, Grace," she continued to cry out.

"Do not speak of him. Do you hear me? I was prepared to do this with little pain to you, but I will torture you by cutting your tongue out if you speak his name again!" I warned.

"She's right, Glory. This is a trap and she is part of it," Finley said. "I know you want to kill her, but you can't. There is a reason."

"I'll kill her," Luther said. Stephanie's eyes widened. She hadn't expected to hear that from him. Hell, I didn't expect it from him either. "In my opinion, all of this is your fault because you just had to have him. He never wanted you, but you manipulated him, keeping him in your grasp. You knew he loved her. Don't get me started on Devin."

"My son! Is my son okay? What did you do to him?" she cried.

"Sister, be calm. Devin is fine. Grace returned him to his father, and they live in Shady Grove now," Astor said with more kindness than any of us could muster.

"Brother, you know all of this started with her. She was supposed to marry you!" she snarled. "If anyone is to blame, it's her. Filthy, trailer trash whore!"

She had flipped a switch from begging me for her life to berating me. Either she was insane or Levi was right and she was playing a game. Fucking Levi was always right, but he didn't know everything.

"So, Dublin, if you are so smart, then tell me what the end game is?" I asked.

"Hell, if I know, Grace," he huffed.

A thundering noise reverberated around the walls. "That

doesn't sound good," Luther said. His wings stretched out behind him, flaring with fire. Troy lifted Driggs, pointing the lighting gun at Stephanie. Levi took his place at my right side, and Dominick stepped up on my left with a pair of pistols. Finley turned to face the door behind us with Astor.

"Mommy's here," Stephanie sing-songed.

The back wall exploded in a cloud of dust and mortar. Centaurs poured into my bathroom, but stayed on the opposite end of the large pool. Marshall entered just before the Queen of Summer waltzed into the room.

"Well, lookie here. Someone let the trash out," Rhiannon smirked.

"Get out of my bathroom," I yelled at her.

She laughed her snide bitchy laugh and shook her head. "Oh, Gloriana, you rush head-long into things without thinking. Did you think you could leave here with the helmet? Along with the pipe dream that you will ever be more than just a banished fairy."

Her words sunk into me. She was right. My father didn't over-turn my sentence. He never had. He only said that I was his heir.

"Oh, you get it now. Daddy couldn't do anything about your banishment. It was the law. Granted he wrote the law, but he never expected his only daughter to defy him," she drolled. "It's too perfect. Standing here in the middle of the inheritance that you can never have, you finally get it. You are no better than Brock-ton. He was banished too. It's why he can't rule this place. Even a marriage to a Summer Queen wasn't enough to break his curse. You will never break yours either. Winter will never be yours."

Brockton walked through the wall to our left flanked by another couple of ogres. If I didn't know better, I could have sworn he had an ogre factory somewhere. He carried a royal blue piece of folded fabric and some black poles. He snapped out the device to reveal a camp chair like the ones that you can fold up in a bag. He sat down, and the ogre to the left handed him a box of popcorn.

"Oh, don't mind me. Carry on," he said, waving at us.

"Brockton! Why is my daughter wearing that helmet?" Rhiannon demanded.

"What part of spectator did you not understand?" he asked her.

"Let her go," she said.

"Please. You never liked her, because she found a way around your obsession with red-headed children," Brock prodded. We stood silently allowing them to talk. Looking through my sight, I saw that Stephanie was held inside the pool with some sort of binding. She couldn't move from that spot. So, partially, she was here against her will or persuaded to do it with incentive, but Brock guaranteed her cooperation with insurance.

"*Do you see the binding?*" I asked Levi.

"*Yes. It's a heavy-duty spell. I don't know if I can break it,*" he said.

"*Don't doubt yourself. That would result in the downfall of us all. Levi pull Winter to you. It will respond. You carry my father's sword. The elements know who you are and will obey,*" I said.

"*Thanks for the pep talk,*" he said. Pretty sure I detected a brood in his tone. I lifted an eyebrow without looking at him. "*Shut up.*" Yep, brood. Yay! At least this trip wasn't a total waste.

"I'm not playing. Thanks, anyway," I said to Brockton as he popped a piece of his snack into his mouth.

"Really?" he asked.

"Yep. Good to see all of you. Especially you Stephanie, I was getting *so worried* about what happened to you," I said, turning my back on all of them.

"No! Grace please don't leave me here!" Stephanie cried. I ignored her, pacing to the door.

"She's bluffing," Brockton said.

I looked at him over my shoulder. "What would a girl like me do with a helmet like that?" I asked.

"Give it to me, Stephanie," Rhiannon said.

"No!" Stephanie yelled. Rhiannon hadn't noticed that she couldn't move, or Rhiannon was in on the ruse. Probably the latter.

"Marshall, get the helmet," Rhiannon ordered.

"Yes, my Queen," he responded. Lowering himself slowly into the pool, the centaur moved toward Stephanie, taking each step with caution. "She is bound."

"Yes, she is! Point for the centaur," Brockton laughed. Were all these fairies bat shit crazy?

"It doesn't matter. Take it!" Rhiannon demanded.

"No! You can't take it off or it will kill me! Please no! Don't take it off!" Stephanie bellowed.

When I made it to the door, I looked back to see Marshall reaching for the helmet. Stephanie's body shook in fear. She looked desperate, and desperate people do stupid things.

"Marshall!" Rhiannon screamed as the centaur hesitated. Brockton practically cackled as he watched Stephanie try to strain away from Marshall. Her face expression changed again. Another flip-flop was coming.

To our right a bright light flashed. I shielded my eyes at its intensity. A long ripping noise spurred me to lower my hand. Through a shimmering rift, I saw my home in Shady Grove. Evening had set in and the lights to the house glowed brightly. Two figures paced on the front porch. Stone and Bronx. Tennyson's guards walked back and forth with large guns. As the rift widened, they stopped their pacing to stare at us which meant they could see the rip. I heard Stone call out to Tennyson who rushed out the front door of the house. Jenny followed on his heels.

"Jenny, get the children," he ordered.

"What did you do!?" I screamed at Stephanie.

"Don't rush her, Grace. Don't play the game," Levi warned. My previous admonition stuck in his head, because I felt him willfully keeping himself from dragging me back.

When I moved to the edge of the pool, Brockton leaned forward smacking on popcorn. "Oh, this is going to be good," he muttered.

Throwing out the Winter power welling up inside of me, the room and bath turned to ice. Stephanie's teeth chittered at the sudden cold.

"You wouldn't release me. You wouldn't help, so I will finish you!" she said.

"Through the rift!" Rhiannon ordered.

Marshall bounded out of the frozen pool throwing shards of ice everywhere. The thundering centaur's hooves filled the small room as they rode through the torn veil. I dashed after them. Levi, instead of holding me back, ran alongside of me. Just as I tried to jump through, the rift shut. Levi hauled me backwards and we landed on the icy floor of the bath. My knights slid to a stop behind me. Stephanie giggled as she watched us tumble to the ground. Brockton roared kicking back in the camp chair and spilling popcorn all over the floor. Even the ogres laughed.

"Levi," I said. He was already standing with Excalibur to open a portal home.

"You might want to wait on that," Brockton warned.

"Nothing keeps me from my children," I said.

"Stephanie, come here," he said.

"Yes, sir," she replied. No longer bound, she waved her hand over the water breaking up the ice inside. She marched up to Brockton, kneeling at his feet. She leaned her helm-covered head into his lap.

"She's such a good little fairy queen," he said, brushing her cheek through the opening of the helm with his hand.

It reminded me of the boy on a leash that Rhiannon had in Summer. Only, Stephanie didn't require a leash or collar. She submitted to him willingly. My skin tingled and my bones vibrated with hatred for her.

"*Gloriana*," Levi called to me. His voice echoed as if he were in a chasm. "*We have to go home.*"

"*The helmet,*" I said.

"*Your children need you,*" he replied.

"I control her, and she controls the helmet," Brock said. "I couldn't put it on since it didn't belong to me. However, she is the daughter of a queen. Honestly, Gloriana, she's better off with the helmet than you. Queen of the Exiles."

"*If we don't take that helmet, we all die,*" I replied, knowing that I might never see my children again, but it would be worth it to stop Brockton.

"Listen to him. You should go spend your last days with your children," Brock smiled. "You have such beautiful children."

"Where is your wife?" I asked. He stopped stroking Stephanie's cheek, grimacing at my question.

"I have no wife," he said.

"I'm sure that you married an ORC," I replied.

"A means to an end. She failed me. I've replaced her with Stephanie," he said. "She has been by my side all along. I cannot fault her too harshly for having a son before she became mine."

"Stephanie, your son is a strong, brilliant young man. Don't you care about him?" I asked. My motherly instinct reached out to hers. However, I found it didn't exist.

"He is better off where he is," she said. I agreed. Especially now, watching her enthralled by my uncle.

"*Make your move. We are with you,*" Levi encouraged.

"*We need Robin,*" I said. "*Finley.*"

"*Damn. I thought I told you to stay out of my head,*" my brother protested.

"*Find Robin,*" I said.

"Screw this, Glory. You and your fucking brilliant ideas. I'm going home," Finley shouted.

Brockton laughed. "He was always a spoiled brat. So much

worse than you, but then again, he didn't completely disregard his father's orders like you did."

The reason for my banishment reared its ugly head again. Time to change the subject.

"Finley, get back here," I ordered. It was a mute order. Verbal only with no magic.

"Fuck off," he growled, stomping off toward my bedroom. "Come on, Astor. You have a wife to get back to."

"Um," Astor hesitated. He looked at me, then somehow caught on. "I'm going with him."

"Go. Don't be in Shady Grove when I get back," I said. "Traitors."

"Seems you have a problem," Brock said.

"No, she doesn't. She has us," Dominick fired back at him. I sure hoped he was crying wolf.

Troy stepped up next to him leveling Driggs at Brock and Stephanie.

"Aren't they Dylan's guns? You gave his guns to your dog?" Brock scoffed.

"I gave his guns to his best friend," I said.

"You realize you can't touch me here," he said, lifting his hand just in front of his body. A shimmering shield appeared as his hand caressed it.

"*I can take it down. Then we rush him. On three,*" Levi said.

"*On your signal,*" I agreed.

Levi's power swelled inside the room. My tattoo began to pulse as he drew more of it to us. The strings on his guitar vibrated with anticipation. Brockton's eyes widened. Fear flashed in his eyes. The bard scared him. Very good.

"*One.*"

"You should know something Brockton, before I kill you," I said, flicking icy blades out from my bare hilts.

"*Two.*"

"What is that, Gloriana?"

"That when I take the throne, you will be forsaken," I said.

He stood, watching Levi as he instructed the ogres to delay us.

"Don't let her leave the room!" I instructed. The command lurched out of my body to Luther, Troy, and Dominick. I saw the slight nod of each head.

"Come, my dear. I've had enough fun for one day," Brockton said preparing to retreat.

"Thr..."

CHAPTER TWENTY-THREE

"Hi, honey, I'm home," Robin cackled as she appeared in the room with us.

"*Is she there?*" Finley asked.

"*Yes, but you stay outside the room. Keep watch. I'll call out to you if we need help,*" I instructed my brother. I wasn't sure where he had found Robin, or how he found her so quickly, but the shocked look on Brockton and Stephanie's faces was priceless.

"Stephanie, please go to my chambers and wait on me," Brockton instructed.

"Um," she said, looking at us, then at Robin. She had two choices on how to leave the room, and she didn't like her chances either way.

"Now!" he commanded. I felt the magical wave pass through us as he forced her to obey.

"Yes, sir," she whimpered. She took tentative steps toward me as she had chosen to avoid the witch on other side of the room. I'd already instructed the guys not to let her leave, plus Finley and Astor were right outside.

"Robin, I can only guess how you got out of your little prison,"

Brockton smirked. "It's unfortunate. I was hoping to enjoy your torture even longer."

"You are going to regret the day you turned on me," she said, flinging balls of fire at him. Each one dissipated as they hit his magical shield.

Stephanie decided it was her moment to bolt. I let her slip past me as I continued inching toward Brockton. Levi stayed close to me as Dominick and Troy pounced on Stephanie.

"No! Don't take it off. I'll die!" she screamed.

Brockton looked over his shoulder where Dominick and Troy had Stephanie pinned on the ground. "She speaks the truth," he said. "Stupid wench took it to manipulate me, but you cannot manipulate a manipulator!"

Yep, they were all bat-shit crazy.

"Let me go!" she squealed.

Robin continued her fruitless onslaught of fireballs. Just before Levi and I got in striking distance, she screamed, "Watch out!" You know, I never understood loyalty. The enemy of my enemy was my friend. No, they were your enemy too!

Brockton spun producing a sword out of thin air. I felt his magic move too late. He swept down at me with a strike that would have severely injured or killed me. Levi tried to react with magic, but even his power had to take a moment to cast. Dominick's wolf shift was faster as he plowed into me. We hit the icy floor hard. He slid past me to a stop.

My armor had a red streak across it.

"Nick!" I screamed knowing I wasn't hit.

Nick still in wolf form rolled over and tried to stand. Blood poured from his leg where his front left paw was severed from his body. He crumpled to the floor shifting back to human.

"Now!" Brockton screamed. The ogres charged Troy and Luther who were holding a writhing Stephanie.

Brockton approached me with his sword raised. Lowering

down upon me, it met the quick work of Levi and Excalibur. Brockton grunted to right himself and squared to Levi.

"Oh, that's right. Bard has a sword. Show me what you've got," Brockton laughed. He started taking swings at Levi.

"Get Nick and get the hell out here," Levi said.

"No, I'm not leaving without you," I said. He grunted as he slammed Excalibur down on Brockton's sword. The tattoo on his arm ignited, and his rock anthem started to play.

I slid myself across the ice to Nick. "Let me see," I said.

"No," he grunted.

"You are losing blood fast," I said, looking at the puddle forming below his hand.

"Leave me," he said. "Just get out of here."

"I'd slap you if you weren't hurt. Finley!" I screamed.

Astor and Finley rushed into the room. "Oh, shit," Finley said.

"Get her out of here," I said, pointing at Stephanie. Finley reached up to her shoulder at the base of her neck and squeezed. She crumpled to the floor. Apparently, my brother had learned my father's sleep pinch.

Troy pointed Driggs at the ogres, making quick work of the oafs. I was glad they didn't have a learning curve when it came to those guns. He and Luther moved over to us. Taking Dominick's shredded shirt, he made a tourniquet for Dominick's arm.

"That's not going to work. We've got to get him back," Luther said.

"He won't even last that long," I said.

"Grace," he muttered. "I can't go back. I'm lamed. The pack won't have me."

"Bull shit. If I say you stay, you stay," Troy countered.

Levi and Brockton traded blows behind us while dodging magical bullets from Robin. She'd changed her tactics. She now threw fire balls and the bricks from the bashed-in wall at Brockton and Levi.

"Cauterize the wound," I said to Luther.

"If you do that, he won't get the hand back," Troy said.

"What? Is he going to grow a new one?" I asked. Perhaps there was some weird shifter regeneration that I hadn't heard of before now.

"No, but maybe the doc can reattach it," he said.

"He is going to bleed out," I argued. Nick's eyes started to fade. I slapped his face, not too hard, but enough to jolt him awake. "You stay awake!"

"Yes, ma'am," he muttered.

"Put something in his mouth. Luther, we need fire," I said.

"I'll give you fire," Robin said hurling a fireball toward us. Luther stretched his wings out to block the flaming orb as it raced toward us. It hit his wings fizzling out. Robin growled in frustration. She started throwing the bricks at us. I pulled power to block the bricks with my own glittering shield. The sapphire heart on my arm pulsed with power.

Brockton hit Levi with a lucky strike, knocking him to his knees. I held my breath for a moment, as Levi righted himself after the blow, then countering Brockton.

"Well done. You've been taught well," Brockton said with admiration in his voice.

"I learned from the best," Levi boasted.

"Tennyson doesn't fight anymore. He's grown weak," Brockton said.

"That's where you are wrong," Tennyson said from the doorway. He held his sword up with a glittering portal just behind him. I cringed for a moment, hoping something terrible didn't happen to him while he was in this room. Having him here was such a risk.

"Fuck," Robin said, darting for the hole in the wall.

"You bitch!" Brockton yelled at her retreat.

Finley and Astor dragged the sleeping Stephanie through the portal.

"Luther, seal that wound before he dies," Tennyson said.

Luther nodded, then his fist turned to a glowing ball like heated steel. Troy grabbed Dominick's wrist pressing it hard against the fist. Dominick's scream ripped through the room. My heart pounded and ached for him as the smell of burned flesh filled the room. His tortured eyes looked at me just before they rolled back in his head.

"Get him home," I ordered.

Troy and Luther lifted him up, moving quickly to the portal.

Tennyson helped me off the floor. I hadn't noticed the tears rolling down my cheeks until he brushed one away. "Get Levi out of here," he said.

"You go through that portal now!" I said.

"I'm not staying here. I'm noble, but not stupid," he said.

Brockton's sword flashed against Levi's again behind us. They were both tiring of the fight. I pushed Tennyson toward the portal. I saw him step through before I started running toward Levi.

"*Position him so that your back is to me,*" I said. Levi didn't acknowledge me, but I saw him shift his feet to put himself between Brockton and me. Brockton started backing him up thinking he had the advantage. Just before I got to Levi, I leaped toward him. "Now!"

I landed square on his back, wrapping my legs around his waist.

"Home!" he yelled as his magic swirled around us.

The Otherworld faded, and we were suddenly standing in my front yard back in Shady Grove. A yard full of centaurs and exiles. I had one of my arms around his neck holding on and riding his back as the gathering stared at us.

"Hi." What else was I supposed to say?

CHAPTER TWENTY-FOUR

Sliding off Levi's back, he turned to me catching my cheek with his palm.

"Are you hurt?" he asked quietly.

"No," I muttered.

"The blood is all his?" he asked.

"Yes, I'm fine," I replied. "I promise. I'm fine. Please go get Tabitha."

With the yard full of centaurs who weren't attacking my home, my attention focused on Levi. He lowered his cheek to mine. His heart pounded in his chest. Turning slightly, he placed a kiss on my cheek.

"I'll be right back," he said, stepping away. Power moved as he disappeared from sight. He knew where Tabitha was based on his connection to the wards and the town. My cheek tingled where he had planted the kiss.

Facing the crowd behind me, I pushed through some observers to see Tennyson and Troy leaning over Dominick who was laying in the grass.

"Levi went to get the doc," I said, kneeling down next to him. "We should take him inside."

"I need to take him home," Troy said. "The pack will handle this."

"He saved my life, and this isn't going to be easy for him. Please take him inside," I pleaded. It wasn't an order. I didn't want to overstep Troy's rule over the pack.

"Alright," he gave in to my request. Luther and Finley hoisted Dominick's limp body, carrying it into the house.

"Mom!" Aydan exclaimed as we walked through the door. He ran up to me, putting his arms around my waist.

"Aydan," I said, brushing his blond locks with my hand. "Where is your sister?"

"She's upstairs. They sealed her room with a ward. Amanda, Mark, and the brownies are with her," he said.

"She needs to stay up there. Nick is hurt, and the doctor is on the way," I said.

"They are taking him to Callum's room?" he asked.

"Yeah. Do you mind sharing with him until we get this sorted out?" I asked.

"That's fine," he said.

I kissed him on the forehead. Callum stood behind him watching the exchange. I couldn't pass him by. My motherly instinct kicked in, and I pulled Callum into a hug.

"You okay too?" I asked.

"Yeah," he blushed.

"Alright," I said, scuffing his hair.

Before I went into the room with Dominick, Troy grabbed my arm. "The decision isn't mine alone. The pack handles things in the old ways. I may be the alpha, but if they vote him out, I can't do anything about it without losing my standing."

"It doesn't matter. He stays in Shady Grove, regardless," I said.

"He's been kicked out of one pack already. It's his story to tell, not mine, but I'm not sure what kind of state of mind he will be in after losing a hand," he said. "Shifting will be fruitless."

"We will find a way to make him whole again," I said. "He saved my life. When you talk to the wolves, you tell them. He sacrificed himself for me which means he did it for them too. Without me in charge here, I doubt the shifters would be allowed to stay."

"I'll try," he said. "I need to go see my family."

"They are upstairs with Winnie. Please keep them up there," I said, as Tabitha turned down the hallway carrying a backpack. Levi followed close behind her. Troy slipped into the room with Dominick.

"What are the centaurs doing?" he asked, pointing at the front door.

Tennyson had been leaning on the side wall of the hallway listening to our conversation. "Marshall was my inside guy. When Rhiannon came through the rift, she decided she was going to go after your children. Marshall and his men backed off. She was pretty pissed when she left, but she left alone."

"That leaves her vulnerable," I said.

"Very," he said with a devious grin very unbecoming of such a noble knight. I loved it.

"She's the key to freeing Shady Grove. Stephanie was right when she taunted me. My father never lifted my banishment. It was given by a joint council. They would have to vote me back in," I said.

"Then we stack the councils in our favor," he suggested.

"I like how you think," I admitted.

"We aren't so different, Grace," he smiled.

A groan from the bedroom brought me back to the dire situation at hand.

"We have to find a way to help him," I said.

"I'll start looking. We owe him that much for taking the hit for you," Levi said. "Go check on him. You might be the only one that can keep him sane and calm through this."

I tilted my head sideways, because it was a generous offer for Levi who didn't like Nick.

"Yeah, whatever. I'm a good guy. Blah, blah," he said.

"You are the best," I replied just before entering the room with Dominick writhing on the bed in pain.

"Levi, we could use a song," I suggested. He didn't come into the room, but from the hallway, he played a soothing tune from the hallway.

"You should have left me. Damn it. I'm useless now," Dominick growled at Troy who was trying to calm him down.

"Troy, go to your family," I said. The statement was laced with power which he clearly felt since his eyes bulged widely.

"Um, you sure?" he asked. I nodded. He rushed past me to get out of the room. I could imagine he was feeling cagey and vulnerable. It could have happened to him.

My eyes landed on Dominick who stared at the window. The curtains were pulled shut, so he was just refusing to look at me. Tabitha moved around the room laying out crystals to cage in healing power. His naked body laid under the sheets with his left arm on top.

"Nick," I said, but it came out not much louder than a whisper.

"Please leave me alone. I want to go home," he said.

I sat down on the edge of the bed. Leaning down over him, I placed a kiss on his cheek. "Thank you, Dominick. I swear to you that we will fix this."

"It can't be fixed," he said.

"And a girl in a trailer park can't be a fairy queen. I'm all about disproving the *can'ts* in this world. Yours is next," I said.

His deep green eyes met mine. "If it were anyone else, I would tell them they were insane. You would do it to spite me."

"Yes, I would," I said with a smile. I saw a hint of light in his eyes for a moment, then it was gone.

CHAPTER TWENTY-FIVE

"Where is she?" I asked.

"Finley has been keeping an eye on Stephanie down at the jail. I saw to it that the security there was increased since Mable escaped," Tennyson said.

We sat inside the office in my trailer. Levi leaned on the desk, listening to the conversation.

"Thank you for taking the risk to get us out," I said.

"I should have gone with you. Grace, I've lived a very long life. The curse of the Forsaken doesn't scare me anymore. Perhaps I'm due that punishment for what I did to your father," he said.

"No, I won't allow it. It's time to move on from those old ways. Seeing Brockton in Winter made me sick. The way he talked and treated people, and the truth is, most of the fairies I used to know acted the same way. I'm not like that, neither are you."

"Thank you, Grace. What do you want us to do with Stephanie?" he asked.

"I want her dead, but she swears if we take off the helmet something crazy will happen. I think she is lying," I said.

"Actually, I was reading in some of the texts that Tennyson

acquired about the helmet. I think you either have to claim your throne to take it and use it. Even if you kill her to get it, you wouldn't be able to use it. I'm concerned that because she technically owns it right now, taking it might cause it to lose it's magic," Levi explained.

I thought for a moment. Was I willing to sacrifice the helmet to kill Stephanie? There were so many people in town on edge that she was still alive and in town. I knew that Brockton wouldn't come after her. Not even for the helmet.

"Maybe we don't need it," I said.

"Let's not make any rash decisions. With its power tied to the veil between worlds, we need to be careful with how we handle this. We don't want to provide Brockton with what he wants," Tennyson warned.

"Do you think that it could happen? That the helmet is not just what helps you see the veil and manipulate it, but it is the power that holds the veil in place?" I asked.

"It would make sense. He wanted you to kill her," Levi said.

"Well, I'll be damned," I muttered.

"I'll see what else I can find out. In the meantime, we need to keep plenty of security on Stephanie. I'll be providing some of my private contractors to help Troy. I suggest that one of the knights be there at all times as well," Tennyson said.

"I'll get with everyone and set up a rotation schedule," Levi said.

"Aren't you just a team leader?" I joked.

Levi shrugged, "And here I thought I was the king."

"You are to me," Tennyson said.

Levi had been joking, but Tennyson was serious.

"Thanks," Levi said.

"Have a good evening. I will be in touch soon," Tennyson said, then exited the office.

"Wow," Levi muttered.

"You've earned your place," I said.

"You see it the same way?" he asked.

"Of course," I said.

Levi's phone rang before he could answer. "Hello."

The voice on the other end sounded like my brother.

"Yes, she is right here. Hang on," Levi said, handing me the phone. "Where is your phone?"

"Left it at home," I said.

"Grace," he scolded. I brushed him off and took the phone from him.

"Hello, Finley."

"Hey, Glory. I wanted to ask a favor," he said.

"Aren't you with Stephanie?" I asked.

"I was, but Astor came to relieve me for a little bit," he explained.

"Oh, okay," I replied. "What do you need?"

"I know you invited me to the family dinner tomorrow, but does that mean Riley is invited too?" he asked. This day was coming no matter how much I dreaded it. Levi nodded.

"Yes, Riley is welcome to come," I replied.

"Wow. I didn't expect that," he said.

"What would you have done if I said no?" I asked.

"I would have told you to fuck off," he replied.

"Love you, too," I responded quickly.

"Thank you, Grace. She's different. I swear it," he said.

"It doesn't matter. It's who you have chosen. I have no say in it," I replied. "But you are still my brother and I love you. It's not about accepting her. It's about loving you."

"See you tomorrow," he said with an excitement in his voice I hadn't heard in a while.

"Bye," I replied, then hung up. "You sure?"

"What you said is true. He's family," Levi replied.

CHAPTER TWENTY-SIX

"Just give me a sign! Anything," I begged, looking up to the trees swaying above me. Their bare branches had prepared for winter. Only a few last holdouts hung precariously shifting in the breeze. It was abnormally warm for November, and I'd gotten lost thinking about the war. I found myself here. Our place. I would have liked to call it that, but we had only been here once.

I kicked at the water in frustration. "Dylan! Is it worth it?" I asked, waiting for a sign. I couldn't go to the stone anymore for fear of running into the Brownie BDSM harem or worse, Lilith. I doubted that he could hear me anyway.

After reflecting on our short jaunt into the Otherworld, we came out of it virtually unscathed. Except for Dominick. His life would never be the same. How many people would die the next time? How many injuries beyond repair? Was this war worth it?

Perhaps my best option was just to protect Shady Grove and my children. Let the Otherworld go into ruin. Let Brockton destroy the veil. We would stay safe here. I could control this.

"You were always here to tell me what to do!" I screamed.

Standing in the center of the creek, where Dylan and I had our last picnic together, I had hoped to find answers. Something to guide me. I felt the urge to right the wrongs. Forgive the forsaken. Restore the exiles. But at what cost?

Who would be next? Whose leg? Arm? Heart? Life?

I buried my face in my hands and pleaded for help. "Just show me the way," I mumbled. The water rushed between my legs with a cool urgency. It wasn't as cold as I expected it to be. However, my frustration had my heart rate up and pounded. I started to cry out again, but then he spoke.

"Grace?"

Levi.

His feet hit the water in a rush, splashing it in different directions. I refused to look up at him, but his arms encircled me.

"What are you doing out here?" he asked.

"Standing in the creek," I mumbled.

"Who were you talking to?" The concern dripped from his voice. His fingers flexed into my back as if they were massaging the answers out of me.

"Him."

"Dylan."

"Yes."

"Did he answer you?"

"Hell no," I muttered. He let out a light laugh. "You didn't take off your shoes," I said still looking down.

"I didn't know what you were doing. They will dry out. Talk to me," he said, lifting my chin.

My eyes met his deep blues. "Levi, you are in the water," I said.

"Um, yeah," he said.

"No, you don't understand. It didn't matter how connected I was to Dylan. I could never get him to lighten up and get in this creek with me. He always had an excuse not to jump in. They were legitimate, but he never took that step. But here you stand," I laughed.

He shook his head. "Grace, I'd follow you anywhere. In the water. To the darkest parts of the Otherworld. Hell, I'd go to war with you."

My breath caught in my throat, and I didn't think. I pressed my lips to his which parted slightly allowing me access. His fingers dug into my back pressing me closer to him, but his lips barely moved. A light caress of his against mine. A vibrating tingle launched through my body like a warm blanket stretching to my toes.

"Grace," he gasped. I withdrew from his mouth, but he held me close, staring into my eyes.

"I got my answer," I said.

"Um, hang on a minute. I'm processing," he said.

I giggled. "Sorry."

"Hell no. Don't be sorry! Ugh! Please, don't be sorry," he said. "Can I do it again?"

"No," I said.

"Why?" he moaned like a lost puppy. I laughed.

"No," I repeated with a smirk. Then pulling the power of the wind stone I throttled that power into my hand, shoving him into the creek. I ran for the bank while his head found the surface of the water.

"Grace Ann Bryant!" he exclaimed. "You are a fucking tease!" He rose up out of the water soaked to the core, then darted out after me.

"Yes, I am," I said, then skipped home.

He was right on my heels as I rushed into the house laughing and running. I burst through the front door, causing Aydan and Callum to jump to their feet.

"Mom!" Aydan exclaimed.

Before I could answer, Levi came barreling into the room dripping water everywhere.

"He's chasing me!" I screamed, running around the room trying to stay away from him.

Aydan and Callum started laughing. Winnie cheered for Levi. The little traitor.

"Get her, Uncle Levi," she yelled.

"Oh, I'm going to get her alright!" Levi grinned.

I squealed as he launched himself toward me, but I ran around the couch. We circled the couch while I protested.

"You are getting the floor, the rug, and everything else soaking wet!" I said.

"Everything?" he asked.

"Not *everything*," I retorted.

"You sure?" he asked, darting around the corner and grabbing my arm. He jerked back hard enough to make me stumble. He caught me, but wrapped me up with his drenched clothes.

"Damn it! I've got to change my clothes now, Levi!" I said.

The kids were laughing as he made an extra effort to rub as much as the water on me as possible.

"That's what you get for shoving me into the creek!" he said.

"You shoved him in the creek?" Aydan asked.

"Maybe," I said.

"That wasn't very nice, Mommy," Winnie said.

"He deserved it," I protested.

"Why? What did he do?" Aydan asked.

Levi and I froze.

"*I kissed her*," Levi said in my head. I gasped for a moment thinking he said it out loud. "*Gotcha!*"

He thought himself quite the comic because he guffawed at the joke.

"Not funny," I muttered. "I'm going to change." I grinned at him, because he couldn't quit laughing.

"But what did he do?" Winnie persisted.

"He was very naughty," I said, stomping off to change my clothes.

"*Might want to change your panties while you are at it,*" he said.

"Very, very naughty!" I continued.

He continued to laugh as I made my way to the bedroom. Once inside, I shut the door, then leaned on the back of it. "Holy shit," I muttered. "What did I just do?"

"*I don't know, but you are going to do it again. Soon!*" he said.

"*Get out of my head!*" I protested.

"*I meant it, Grace. Kiss or no kiss. I'd follow you anywhere,*" he said.

If this was Dylan's version of an answer, it was definitely twisted. I could almost hear him laughing. I'm sure there was an "I told you so" somewhere in there.

Aydan and I sat on the front porch drinking lemonade after I'd changed into dry clothes while Callum in wolf form chased Winnie through the yard. Rufus stood at the window inside barking at them.

"Hush, Rufus! I'll let Callum eat you," I said.

"Mom, you never talked to me about what happened with Atohi," he said.

"I've been kinda busy," I replied. "Do you want to talk about it?"

"I just know that I felt inside of me the need to make it right again. It was my responsibility," he explained.

"Your father felt the same way about things sometimes," I said.

"So, it's the Thunderbird in me," he surmised.

"Yes. I'm proud of you for sticking up for Callum," I said.

"It's nice to have a friend. After we talked about what happened with Atohi, I knew I would help him in whatever way I could," he said.

"Did he tell you what happened in the ring with Athoi?" I asked.

"Yep. He said that he had always done what Atohi said because they were both Native American, and Atohi was his elder. He didn't know that Atohi wanted to kill him," he said.

I kissed him on the cheek. "I'm proud of you, Aydan. Dylan would be proud of you too," I said.

"Thanks, Mom," he said as he watched Callum chasing Winnie.

Winnie took to Callum very quickly. I supposed it was her friendship with Mark which made her accept him into the household. I'd gained another child. At least Callum was grown. Well, mostly.

Later today, we would take Dominick back home. He lived alone in a small farmhouse just down the road from Troy and Amanda. We were only waiting on the final vote from the werewolves on whether he would be accepted back into the pack. His mental state wavered over the last few days. The impending vote would determine whether he recovered fully or not.

"Where's Uncle Levi?" Aydan asked.

"He went to town for something. He's up to no good," I said.

"Mom." His voice was quiet, but not a whisper.

Looking down at him, his bright blue eyes met mine. "What is it?"

"I'm sorry I grew up so fast," he said.

I grinned. "Aydan, that wasn't your fault. You have no reason to apologize. I love you all the same. You are the part of Dylan that I got to keep. That and your sister's fiery explosions."

He smiled at that. "She's a hot mess," he said.

"Well put!"

"I wish I could have known him," he said.

"He was the best thing that ever happened to me, but now you are," I said. "So, I have to be thankful for what I have instead of the years that were never meant to be. Besides, you will always be my baby boy."

"I love you, Mom," he said, hugging me from the side.

I wrapped my arms around him and kissed the crown of his head.

"Go chase the wolf and phoenix. I'm going to check on Nick," I said.

After putting our empty glasses in the sink, I made my way down to the room where Nick stayed. I could never convince him to come out even just to watch television with us. The door was open, but I knocked.

"Come in, Grace," he said.

He sat across the room in a soft velvet wing chair. He was wearing a green and black plaid shirt and jeans. I sat down on the bed with my legs folded under me.

"How are you today?" I asked.

"I'm fine," he replied shortly.

"Can I get anything for you?" I asked.

"No," he said.

"Do you want me to leave you alone?"

He hesitated. "No."

"You thinking about the vote?"

"I am."

"It will be fine. If they don't take you back, then you can stay here. I need someone to work on our security at the house. The magic is one thing, but we need guards. The centaurs have volunteered, but they've taken up residence at Dylan's old farm. The house is gone, but the barn is still there. Marshall played both sides even though he was Tennyson's informant. I need someone that I know is on my side," I said. Levi and I discussed it and we thought that Nick would be the best person for the job.

"How am I supposed to do that with one hand?" he asked.

"Not be a bitter twat and get up off your ass," I said.

His eyes flared with anger. I started laughing at him, then he broke a smile.

"I'm not a twat," he said.

"Yes, you are. I love it when Levi broods, but it doesn't look good on you," I said.

His face sobered, and I saw his lip quiver for a moment. He reigned it in though.

"I've never been a part of anything. My father hated me from the moment I was born. My mother was not his mate. His mate, after many years of trying couldn't produce a child for him. So, reluctantly, with his wife's permission, he participated in an artificial insemination in order to create a child. Me. My real mother gave me up to him without any payment. He was the alpha, and she was proud that her son would be one too. She didn't want me. She wanted the prestige. It wasn't long after I was born that my step-mother became pregnant. It was a rough pregnancy, and she and the child died. My father mourned for them, as he should have. I was young and didn't understand. As I got older, he resented me. I became rebellious and hated the fact that I was his son. Like any rejected teenager, I did whatever I could to make his life miserable. Eventually, he cast me out. With no heir, he was challenged and defeated as Alpha. I roamed until one day while sitting in a bar in Steelshore. The television above the bar showed a beautiful woman leaving a courtroom where she was being accused of murder."

"Oh, good grief," I moaned. "Seriously?"

"No lie. I saw it all go down. The struggle to get you to the car. You hiding behind Levi. The camera even caught Dylan as he died. Of course, I didn't know he was the Phoenix," he said.

"At that point, neither did I," I said.

"Really?"

"Really. There were a lot of things I didn't know then that I do now. I'm a different person," I said.

"Well, I saw you faint. I could have sworn the man behind you made you faint. I had a gut feeling that you were being coerced in the situation," he said.

He had seen my father, Oberon, put me to sleep with a pinch to my neck. "So, you came here to rescue me?"

"Not exactly," he said. "I moved to Birmingham."

"Well, that didn't go as I expected," I laughed.

"I mean, you were beautiful, but what was I going to do with a woman accused of murder? Anyway, while I was in Birmingham, I saw the reports that you were acquitted. A man in a coffee shop saw me reading the newspaper with the article in it. He was an imposing man with tattoos peeking out from under his very expensive suit," he explained.

"Tennyson," I said.

"Yeah. He saw me reading the article, and for some reason, he decided to talk to me. He suggested that I check out Shady Grove. He flatly said that I would find more of my kind there. I was astonished that he knew what I was."

"He has a lot of gifts. He knows a lot of things," I replied.

"I had nothing to lose. I wasn't here a whole day when Troy approached me. A wolf knows a wolf. I started hanging out at his house, but kept out of town. I didn't want anyone to know who I was. My previous life as wolf wasn't a good experience. I refused to meet any other shifters. Troy would talk about you and Dylan, and the day he came and told me that Dylan died was rough for him. Amanda comforted him as much as she could, but he took it hard. Troy loved Dylan like a brother. I decided that he needed a friend to fill that void and became determined to make sure it was me. The first time I ever saw you in person was in the field the day we found the eyeless man on patrol. I saw the connection then between you and Levi. Then Dylan died. I didn't approach you because I thought that I needed to fill that hole in you. I approached you because you were strong. You continued your job protecting this realm despite your grief. You were raising your children."

"I did what any mother would do," I said.

"No, my mother didn't. When I was banished, I tried to reach out to her. She wouldn't even return my calls. No, not all mothers are good mothers," he said.

This was very true. Bethany Jones had tried, but her addictions superseded the need to provide a stable home for Winnie. Stephanie wanted nothing to do with Devin. I couldn't understand it, because my children were everything to me.

Nick continued, "I tried one last time at the wedding, but I saw you with Levi. There is a connection there that I could never have with you, and I accept that."

"Would working for me here cause you pain?" I asked.

He laughed, "Grace, I'd be honored to be the man in your life, but I'm not going to die if I don't get you."

"Well, my ego just deflated," I said.

"But I will be lost if the pack doesn't accept me. I need them. I need that acceptance from my own kind. After finally letting them into my life, I can't imagine what it would be like to be alone. I don't know how Troy did it all those years. Callum being here is good for him. He's young and unattached. I'm not," he said sadly. His eyes lifted to the doorway. With my senses, I knew Levi was home. "Hey, Levi."

"Hey, Nick. Troy is here," he said.

"Alright," he said, pushing himself up out of the chair with his right hand.

We walked into the living room where Troy and Amanda waited. I couldn't tell anything by their expressions.

"Hey," Troy said.

"Hello," Nick replied.

The tension in the room settled on my chest. It was heavy, and I heaved a sigh trying to release it. Levi's arm wrapped around my waist, and I leaned into him.

"The wolves and I talked for a long time. We left it alone for a couple of days, then approached it again last night. The meeting lasted all night, and I've had very little sleep," Troy said. "I won't lie to you, Dominick. It was a battle. I have sworn my allegiance to you as my Beta. My survival as Alpha depends upon you reintegrating into the pack with no issues. You will be tested, and often, I would guess, but you are still my Beta. The pack accepts you as you are."

Dominick's face twisted with emotions. "I don't want to put you in jeopardy," he said.

"It's too late. You are part of my family, and I won't give you up," Troy said.

Tears rolled down my cheeks. "Damn," I muttered, wiping them away. Levi squeezed me tighter to his side.

Dominick plodded across the room with heavy footsteps and fell into the awaiting arms of his friend and Alpha. "Thank you," he groaned. "I won't make you regret it."

Troy patted him on the back. "Yeah, you better not," he laughed.

"Come home," Amanda said.

Dominick turned and looked at me with a wide grin. "Thank you, Grace."

"I didn't do anything," I said.

"I laid a bunch of shit on you in there," he said, pointing with his stub arm. "Fuck. I forget I don't have a hand to point."

I started to laugh, but covered my mouth. Troy laughed though, so I figured it was okay.

"I'm always here if you need to talk," I saidm smiling at him.

The light had returned to his eyes which made me determined to find a fix for him. Until we found a way to get him balanced as a wolf, he would not shift. The pack would expect it eventually. Levi was already researching methods to come up with a solution. I had faith that we would find something. Until then, I had no doubt that Dominick would prove to be the best partner Troy could have. Hand or no hand.

CHAPTER TWENTY-SEVEN

Gathered around the table with our family, we shared a dinner like Thanksgiving. Someone told me that Thanksgiving shouldn't be celebrated because of the basis with the First People and the Europeans, but the heart of Thanksgiving was sharing with family. And in the South, good food.

We didn't have turkey though. I made spaghetti.

"This is so good," Callum said.

"I told you," Winnie smirked.

"It's awesome. My mom is the best," Aydan beamed.

I was blessed to have him as a baby, but now his adoration as a teen warmed my heart in ways that I never expected, much like his father had done. Across the table from me, Nestor sat having a deep discussion about the finer points of liquor with William. Bramble and Briar perched themselves on a bookshelf across the room enjoying cups of milk with vanilla wafers. Rufus sat at my feet. He had actually allowed Callum to pet him today which was progress for the mutt.

"Thanks for having me, Grace. It is wonderful," Riley said. She had been quiet most of the night, sticking close to Finley. She talked mostly to William and Nestor. Finley seemed nervous, but he had relaxed once he realized that we were serious about accepting her for his sake.

"Oh, I meant to show you this," Finley said, digging in his pocket. He pulled out a plastic card and handed it across Levi to me. I looked down at the driver's license issued by the state of Alabama. It belonged to Finley Bryant.

"Bryant?" I said with a smile.

"You are my sister. We should have the same last name. Well, that is until you get married," Finley said, nudging Levi with his elbow. Levi brushed him off, refusing to play the game with him.

"This is awesome," I said, handing him back the identification card.

"I know. I'm awesome," he said.

By my side, Levi sat patting his full belly. "Damn, I think I'm going to have to have another," he said.

"Another plate?" I asked, because he had piled the last one pretty high.

"No, another beer," he said.

"Piss water," I groaned.

"Go get it for me," he said, kicking my foot under the table.

Everyone stopped moving and talking waiting for my response.

"I am *not* your maid, Dublin," I said.

"No, but you are hosting this dinner, and I demand my just hospitality," he smirked, pushing my limits.

"Levi Rearden," I huffed. "I am not going to get you another beer."

"I'm pretty sure you are required since you decided to have this dinner," he continued.

"I am going to jerk a knot in your tail!" I yelled losing my patience. I had thought he was joking, but clearly, he wasn't.

"Pretty sure you owe me ten bucks, Dad," Levi said.

"What?" I asked.

"Indeed, I do," William replied, digging in his pocket for his wallet.

"You bet him that I would say it," I said, realizing the game.

William handed him a ten-dollar bill. Levi snapped it tight between his hands. Then handed it to Winnie. "Here you are, Princess. Buy yourself something nice."

"Thank you, Uncle Levi," Winnie said with wide eyes. She took the money from him and stuffed it into her pocket.

"Ass," I muttered, gathering my plate from the table to take to the kitchen.

The conversation at the table resumed as I stood up, stalking off to the kitchen. I knew he would follow me.

"I thought you were in a good mood," he said.

"I was until you tried to make a fool of me," I huffed.

"I didn't have to try very hard," he smirked.

I rounded on him with my hand in the air. He caught my wrist with a grin. "Were you going to slap me?" he asked playfully.

"You are being an ass," I said.

"I am. You could spank me. I'd like that more than a slap," he said.

"Levi!" I said, trying to jerk my hand away from him. Heat rose to my neck and cheeks. He wouldn't let go. He backed me up step by step to the kitchen counter.

"Gloriana," he said.

"Stop using that name," I whispered, looking over his shoulder to make sure no one else could see us.

"Why? It's your name. It feels right. Just like this," he said, picking up a blonde curl from my shoulder. He twirled it around his finger. My heart pounded in my chest. My emotions swirled in fifty directions. He moved closer, wrapping his arm around my waist. "I'm sorry. I was only playing." He kissed the palm of my hand, then let my wrist go.

"Hmph," I said, turning my face from his.

"Please forgive me," he said, kissing my cheek. I felt his hot breath and the pounding of his heart. He was unsure of what he was doing, but he was doing it anyway. The rush of attraction and admiration displayed with an embrace and a touch of his lips. I may have whimpered at the intensity of it. Okay, I whimpered, but the fairy inside of me trembled with anticipation. "You were happy today. It was so good to see you happy again."

"What's your middle name?" I asked.

"Is that the condition for forgiving me?" he asked.

"Yes," I said.

"Oh, well," he said, kissing me on the cheek again, then moving away. Part of me died when all he kissed was my cheek. The other part protested the thought. I was an emotional mess around him now. It was hard to tell the difference between desire and devotion. "Guess I'm in the dog house."

"What?!" I exclaimed.

He grinned, then darted into the dining room. "Get these dirty dishes picked up off this table. We gotta clean up if we are going to get a Christmas tree tomorrow. You, youngins will have to be up early, bright-eyed and bushy-tailed!"

NOTE FROM THE AUTHOR

Thank you so much for reading the 10th installment of the Fairy Tales of a Trailer Park Queen. By now, these characters are so engrained in me that I don't know what I'm going to do when the story ends. I've had so many ask about how many books are left. The plan is for 15 books plus a short story anthology focused on the minor beloved characters in Shady Grove.

Now I've decided to do a spin-off series that will focus on Wynonna Riggs, Grace's Phoenix Daughter. Winnie will be a young adult in the series called Stories of Frost and Fire. It will be a five-book series with a prequel. I will start writing those next year.

My next project is to write another prequel for Fairy Tales of a Trailer Park Queen which will be included in a FREE anthology of fantasy and urban fantasy works with other wonderful authors. It will be released in February of 2019.

I'm also testing narrators for the release of the audio versions of Fairy Tales of a Trailer Park Queen sometime next year.

All my updates, teasers, and giveaways take place in my reader group, Magic and Mason Jars. Join us for all the fun and sass: https://www.facebook.com/groups/KSwainMagicandMasonJars/

Also, please take the time to leave an honest review of the book either on Amazon, Goodreads, or Bookbub. I really appreciate it.

The next book is Bright-Eyed and Bushy-Tailed. You can purchase it HERE.

Thanks again, and bless your heart. (I mean that in the good way. I promise.)

CHARACTER LIST

Grace Ann Bryant- Exiled fairy queen hiding in Shady Grove, Alabama. Daughter of Oberon. Also known as Gloriana, to her Father and the fairies of the Otherworld. She was called Hannah while traveling with the gypsy fairies before coming to North America. Owns a dachshund named Rufus. Loves orange soda and Crown. Nickname: Glory

Dylan Riggs- Deceased. Sheriff of Loudon County, Alabama. Fiancé to Grace Ann Bryant. The last living Thunderbird and the only living Phoenix. Also known as Serafino Taranis and Keme Rowtag. Nickname: Darlin'

Levi Rearden- Changeling from Texas brought to live with Grace by Jeremiah Freyman. Given Bard powers by Oberon. Given Excalibur by the Lady of the Lake. Looks good in a towel. Nickname: Dublin

Wynonna Riggs- formerly known as Wynonna Jones, but

adopted by Grace and Dylan. Human daughter of Bethany Jones who dies in Tinsel in a Tangle. Given the power of the Phoenix by her father. Nickname: Winnie, Wildfire

Aydan Thaddeus Riggs- son of Dylan Riggs and Grace Ann Bryant. Heir to Thunderbird inheritance. By the end of Fuller than a Tick, Aydan is approximately 16 years old which is old enough to produce an heir. Given the Native American name, Yas Shikoba meaning "snow feather." He is a white raptor when in Thunderbird form.

Nestor Gwinn- Grace's maternal grandfather. Kelpie. Owner of Hot Tin Roof Bar in Shady Grove. Maker of magical coffee.

Troy Maynard- Police chief in Shady Grove. Wolf shifter. Married to **Amanda Capps** and father to his adopted son, **Mark Capps** (Maynard) who is Winnie's best friend. Given Driggs, Dylan's guns, by Grace.

Betty Stallworth- wife to Luther Harris. Waitress at the diner. Flirts with everyone. Banshee.

Luther Harris- head cook at the diner. Part of Grace's war council. Ifrit.

Tabitha Mistborne- fairy physician. Daughter of Rhiannon. Dating Remington Blake.

Mable Sanders- former spy for Oberon. Fairy Witch. Former girlfriend of Nestor Gwinn. One of three witches known as the Order of the Red Cloak (ORC).

Sergio Krykos- Grace's Uncle who has taken over the Other-world. In his first life, he was known as Mordred, half-brother to King Arthur. Goes by the name Brockton.

Oberon- Deceased. King of the Winter Otherworld. Grace's father. In his first life, he was known as King Arthur.

Rhiannon- Queen of the Summer Otherworld. Half-sister to Oberon. In her first life she was known as Morgana, a fairy witch.

Remington Blake- Grace's ex-boyfriend. Dating Tabitha Mist-borne. From N'awlins. Sweet talker. One of the Native American Star-folk.

Astor- The ginger knight that Grace brought back from the Summer realm. Formerly betrothed to Grace. Former First Knight of the Tree of Life. In his first life, he was Percival, Knight of the Round Table. Engaged to Ella Jenkins.

Callum Fannon- the white wolf taken in by Grace during FTAT. Approximately 18 years old. Becomes friends with the now grown Aydan.

Dominick Meyer- Beta wolf to Troy Maynard. Loses hand in the battle of the Helm protecting Grace. Accepted back into the pack. Crushes on Grace.

Matthew Rayburn- Druid. Spiritual leader of Shady Grove. Leads services in a Baptist Church which is a portal into the Summer Realm. Enthralled by Robin Rayburn. Now blind after being cursed by Robin.

Kadence Rayburn- Daughter of Matthew. Ex-girlfriend of Levi. Enthralled by Malcom Taggert. Becomes a fairy. Dating Caleb Joiner. Part of the three white witches to counter the ORCs.

Malcolm Taggart- Deceased. Incubus that once tried to seduce Grace. Enthralls Kady.

Caleb Joiner- Lives with Malcom and Kady, but frees Kady from Malcolm.

Riley McKenzie- Daughter of Rhiannon and Jeremiah Freyman. Levi's ex-girlfriend. Stole the songbook. Fled the Summer Realm with Grace. Living with Finley, Grace's brother. Part of the three white witches to counter the ORCs.

Stephanie Davis- Daughter of Rhiannon. Dylan's ex-girlfriend. Sergio Krykos' ex-girlfriend. Mother to Devin Blankenship. Found in the Otherworld wearing the Helm of Arthur, Goswhit.

Joey Blankenship- Tryst with Grace. Enthralled by Stephanie. Father to Devin Blankenship. Turned into a faun by Rhiannon. Escapes the Summer Realm with Grace and his son.

Eugene Jenkins- Mayor of Shady Grove. Former Knight of the Round Table, Ewain. Wife died in childbirth. Father to Ella Jenkins. Partner to Charles "Chaz" Leopold.

Eleanor "Ella" Jenkins- Changeling daughter of Mayor Jenkins. Catches Astor's eye. Teacher at the fairy school.

Charles "Chaz" Leopold- Also known as "The Lion." Hairdresser. Second Queen in Shady Grove.

Finley Bryant- Grace's "twin" brother. Once married to Nelly, but now is living with Riley McKenzie. Wears armor portraying the symbol of Grace's royalty.

Jenny Greenteeth- A grindylow living in Shady Grove. In her first life, she was known as Guinevere, wife of Arthur, lover of Lancelot. Cursed to her current form.

Tennyson Schuyler- Mob boss. In his first life, he was known as Lancelot, Knight of the Round Table. Oberon calls him Lachlan.

Cletus and Tater Sawyer- Last human residents of Shady Grove. Comical, but full of heart.

Yule Lads- A group of Christmas Trolls who moved into town. Lamar is the most frequently mentioned with his various peg legs. Others include: Phil, Cory, Willie, Chad, Keith, Kevin, Phillip, Ryan, Bo, Richard, and Taylor.

Michean Artair- Solomonar. Owner of Magic Vape. Produces magical liquids for all occasions.

Brittany Arizona- Shady Grove's tattoo artist.

Bramble and Briar- Brownies who live in Grace's house, but are attached to Winnie. Hired by Caiaphas to watch over Grace. Now in servitude to Grace. Kinky little fairies.

Caiaphas- Leader of the now defunct Sanhedrin. Former Knight of the Round Table.

Fordele and Wendy- King and Queen of the Wandering Gypsy Fairies. Fordele was Grace's lover ages ago. Wendy leads the three white witches to combat the ORCs. Ford has moved our of their RV for unknown reasons in FTAT.

Josey- Grace's former neighbor in the trailer park. Perpetually pregnant. Goddess of the Tree of Life. Also known as Lilith. Also known to be a little bit unstable.

Jeremiah Freyman- Deceased. Former member of the Sanhedrin that brought Grace, Dylan, Levi, and most of the other fairies to Shady Grove. Worked for Oberon. Father of Riley. Former Knight of the Round Table. Known as Tristan.

Deacon Giles- Farmer in Shady Grove. Krampus.

Connelly Reyes- First Knight of the Fountain of Youth. Former Knight of the Round Table known as the Grail Knight, Galahad. Best friends with Astor.

Chris Purcell- Winged-werehog. Known as a dealer of information. Settled in Shady Grove with his domesticated wife, **Henrietta**.

Lissette Delphin- Creole Priestess. Tricked Levi into summoning the demon, Shanaroth. Speculation that she is the 3rd witch in a triad called the Order of the Red Cloak (ORCs).

Rowan Flanagan- Partner of Tennyson Schuyler. Died in Summer Realm. Mother of Robin Rayburn. In her first life, she was known as Elaine. Mother of Galahad.

Atohi- midnight wolf, Cherokee Native American shifter like Dylan. Appears to want to help Grace. Participates in the blessing of Aydan to receive his father's inheritance.

OTHER MINOR CHARACTERS

Kyffin Merrik- Former partner in Sergio Krykos law firm. Missing.

Demetris Lysander- Grace's former lawyer. Deceased. Aswang.

Phillip Chastain- Judge at Grace's hearing in BYH. Helps with legal matters. Liaison to Human Politicians.

Misaki- Oni disguised as a Kitsune.

Elizabeth Shanteel and Colby Martin- human children murdered in BYH by Demetris Lysander.

Rev. Ezekiel Stanton- Pastor of Shady Grove Church of God. Evacuated when the humans left Shady Grove.

Sylvestor Handley- Michael Handley's father. Blacksmith.

Diego Santiago- Bear shapeshifter. Executed by Grace.

Juanita Santiago- Bear shapeshifter. Widow. Mother of two. Oversees a farm with Deacon Giles help.

Niles Babineau- Developer from New Orleans that helped Remington Blake build more housing in Shady Grove. Returned to New Orleans.

Jessica- Summer fairy working at the sheriff's office.

Stone and Bronx- Tennyson Schuyler's bodyguards.

Eogan- Treekin in Summer Realm.

Marshall- Captain of the Centaurs in Summer Realm.

Nimue- Lady of the Lake. Keeper of Excalibur. Controls the Water Element Stone.

Brad and Tonya- Brad owns the BBQ joint in Shady Grove. Tonya works there as a waitress.

Katherine Frist- Fairy woman living in Shady Grove known for her many dead husbands.

Ellessa- Grace's Siren mother. Whereabouts unknown.

Melissa Marx- Levi fangirl.

Taliesin- Bard for Arthur and many other Kings and Rulers. Wrote the songbook given to Levi.

Thistle- Purple haired pixie with a love envelope.

Sandy- Matthew Rayburn's Nurse.

Phelan and Ingo- two wolves fighting in the ring at the Wolves Fight Club.

Sammy- Wolf guard at the Wolves Fight Club.

Chaytan, Talako, Hosa- three native American shaman who came to bless Aydan with his father's Thunderbird inheritance.

ACKNOWLEDGMENTS

A lot of this book focuses on the wolf pack in Shady Grove. Rufus is mentioned quite a few times. I have my own Rufus, but his name is Kaiser. He has a younger, but bigger brother named Carter. Our furbabies brighten our lives each day. This book is dedicated to the creatures that warm our souls.

I'd like to thank Carol, Erica, and Hampton for their professional work. Thanks to Audrey who took on the rebrand for the series and has done a wonderful job.

I'd like to acknowledge my BETA and ARC teams. You guys are fabulous and make my work look better.

I attended the 20booksto50k conference in Las Vegas this year and met a ton of fabulous authors. It was so great to put faces to the names I already knew. Thanks especially to John, Ben, and Orlando who were enthusiastic with helping me further my writing career. Thanks to Luke, Ramy, and Robyn for a car ride I'll never forget. Thanks to Tabitha for being my plus one.

As always, I'm so thankful for my family. My parents, in-laws, grandparents, and friends who have supported and believed in me. I love you, Jeff and Maleia.

From early in life Kimbra Swain was indoctrinated in the ways of geekdom. Raised on Star Wars, Tolkien, Superheroes and Voltron, she found herself immersed in a world of imagination. She started writing in high school, and completed her English degree from the University of Alabama in 2003.

Her writing is influenced by a gamut of authors including Jane Austen, J.R.R. Tolkien, L.M. Montgomery, Timothy Zahn, Kathy Reichs, Kevin Hearne and Jim Butcher.

Born and raised in Alabama, Kimbra still lives there with her husband and 5-year-old daughter. When she isn't reading or writing, she plays PC games, makes jewelry and builds cars.

Join my reader group for all the latest updates on releases, fabulous giveaways, and launch parties.

Follow Kimbra on Facebook, Twitter, Instagram, Pinterest, and GoodReads.
www.kimbraswain.com

CPSIA information can be obtained
at www.ICGtesting.com
Printed in the USA
LVHW041030040520
654954LV00002B/516

9 781791 961